New H

New Neighbours

By Ted Bun

December 2017

DEDICATION

To

My friends and neighbours in the UK and
France.

I would like to say a big thank you to Susan Randle for permission to use her photograph.

This story is fictional.

The characters are not intended to reflect any living person. If you think you are featured, drop me a line. I like my characters!

I hope you enjoy the story...

Ted

Index

Hi, I'm Jerry

We finally moved into our new cottage on the edge of the village of Les Lilas on 23rd March. We had driven down from the Channel Tunnel over the weekend, keen to move in on Monday.

How remiss of me, introductions first. I'm Jerry, Jerry Tilson and my beautiful wife is Francene, Fran to you and me. We have both just retired, well sort of, from working in one of England's most respected major teaching hospitals. It wasn't so much we retired as we saw the changes coming down the line at us, grabbed our pension pots and ran. We paused only long enough to sell up in the UK, find a nice house in France and serve our notice period.

Back to our story;

Nine-fifteen and there we were, standing on the doorstep of the office of our immoblier, as they (appropriately) call an estate agent in France. They don't get much more immobile than Mme Slade. Our meeting was scheduled for 8:30, she was, as ever, late.

To date, Mme Slade, a lady of Scottish extraction via London, had done little, apart from pocketing a cheque for several thousand euro. What she had done to earn such riches eluded us both. Apart from booking an appointment for us to see the house. She arrived at our rendezvous twenty minutes late on that occasion. Mme Slade had then left it to the vendors to show us around while she looked at her watch and tutted.

She arrived at her office and handed over the huge bunch of keys to our French paradise, half past nine. We were only an hour behind schedule, after just one hour. Time to start worrying about the rest of the project plan. I was, for my sins, a Project Manager in my old life.

As a consequence of that hour slippage, we were late getting to our new house. The lads in the furniture van had another job to drop off that afternoon. Rather than waste time waiting, they had taken matters into their own hands. We arrived in time to find that most of our furniture was already in the front garden. We got the door open and at the lads' suggestion started moving the furniture into the house. They carried on getting the rest of our worldly goods out of their waggon and onto the gravel of our driveway. Fortunately, they were ahead of their schedule when the van was emptied of all our chattels. In exchange for a generous tip, they stayed long enough to help with the heaviest bits of furniture, before they took off towards the distant Pyrenees, leaving us to sort out the remaining boxes and bags.

Several hours and layers of knuckle skin later, our precious possessions were undercover. We had no phone, no internet and, most important of all, no food. This situation was allowed for in the project plan. Accordingly, we set off to the café bar in the village square. We ordered a pizza each, a pitcher of the house red wine and the 'wiffy' code. We cranked up the laptop and opened the deluge of e-mails. That is if you can call four erectile dysfunction cures, one Nigerian financial offering and a bevvy of Ukrainian girls offering their rather youthful bodies to me a deluge.

Fran fared rather better with 'good luck in your new home' messages from both of our kids, her sister, both of my sisters and half a dozen from former colleagues. In addition, she had received five 'when can we come and stay?' messages, only one was in both groups. Plus, her usual selection of shopping-

3

related messages and two Nigerians wanting help with emptying our bank account.

It was still early, much too early for bed, so we had another jug of plonk. As that jug was progressively draining itself, we made our first important discovery, the locals did not use any of the words we had learnt in our school French lessons. They could just about understand what we said, but we couldn't make out a word of what they were saying. It was like a Londoner (me) trying to have a conversation with a Glaswegian. They got what the 'posh London twit' (me, again) was saying from watching TV. They, on the other hand, tend to speak an argot, with a thick accent, that your average UK Southerner has never heard before.

A little later, we made another one. It is dark along the road leading back to our new home. Not just the absence of daylight, but of any light. Street lights are not part of the street furniture and neither are white lines. Thankful for a powerful, modern smartphone, we found our way without treading on or in anything too awful en route. I am continually amazed that Apollo 11 took men to the moon with a mere sixty-four kilobits of computer power and it takes a full thirty-two gigabits for us to find our way home in the dark! Obviously, the pioneering spirit of the American people lasted into the space age!

We were also able to find the keyhole in the front door using the same highly sophisticated piece of technology. What it couldn't help with was finding the electric plug adaptors, so that we could plug our British kettle into the French socket. Nor could it help us find the matches to light the gas stove to heat a saucepan of water. They had been put somewhere safe, somewhere where we can find them later, somewhere where they will be easy to find or they were still hiding in one of the many boxes.

"Hence," as a greater diarist than I could ever hope to be said, "to bed."

Our first night in our own home in France was peaceful. Rather too peaceful. Where was the traffic noise? The late-night revellers kicking a tin down the road? Surely an ambulance or police car should have dashed passed, siren blaring.

All I could hear was Fran's gentle breathing as she slept through that night of fearful sounds. The continual tap, tap,

tap on the windows. The rattle that sounded like someone trying to get in through the kitchen door. The blood-curdling screams that echoed around the garden. Which, all combined to make my two emergency trips, in the blackness, to the bathroom, a truly frightening journey.

Fran, pleased to meet you

My goodness, the first night in our new house. I hardly slept at all. What with Jerry crashing around, tossing, turning, farting and snoring, but apart from that, it was really peaceful. Oh, and his trips to the bathroom, at least I hope he found the bathroom. He was slightly, how should I put it, pissed out of his tree. We had ordered two 'demis' of wine and a couple of beers. Apart from one (small) beer and about a glass and a half of the local red, he had drunk the lot. On the good side, he had held it together while we were in the bar, it will be, 'the fresh air that caused it!' and he didn't sing.

I lay in bed listening to the sounds of the morning and reading while the blob next to me started to make it's early morning sounds and movements. A few juddering snorks, a couple of hunches and then the scratching of the pubes to indicate a return to the world.

I'll give him his due, he did try to hide the pain behind his eyes and got up to make the coffee. Why making coffee involved the opening and closing the bathroom cabinet and the fridge, several times, was not obvious, until some half an hour later, Jerry arrived bedside with my coffee. It was obvious that the paracetamol washed down with a pint of water, no make that milk, the tell-tale dribbles from the milk carton were still visible at the corner of his mouth.

He climbed back into bed, rummaged around for his tablet computer and turned it on. After another five minutes of muttering and cursing, he rolled his eyes in despair.

"Of course, we do not have the internet yet!"

I just smiled, it pays not to hint at, nor give the merest suggestion of, 'I could have told you that,' let alone 'I told you so', to Jerry. I just leave it for him to find out for himself, or I sneak off and secretly solve it myself. I believe it is called 'man management.'

We lay together, alternately reading and talking about the day to come. The last of the coffee had gone cold in the bottom of my cup. I'm a shocker for only drinking the top two-thirds of a cup of coffee or tea. I blame my big sister for that, giving me a cup of tea straight from the pot when I was about five or six. The feel of the resulting mouthful of tea leaves has never left me. To this day I can't drink the bit at the bottom of a cup. I handed my remaining coffee to Jerry, who knocked it back.

"That's gone cold very fast, what time is it?"

I looked at my phone, before passing on the fact it was nearly nine. We had been idling in bed for over an hour! No wonder the coffee had gone cold.

Jerry leapt, well that's what he called it, out of bed, then bounded across the room, see my previous comment, and threw open the shutters. Well, almost, I'd have said that they groaned open on their rusted hinges but I was too busy chortling to myself as the sun streamed in through the open French windows, illuminating Jerry in all his naked finery.

Much to my disappointment, there were no male shouts of anger nor shrieks of female terror, nor for that matter laughs and calls of amusement. I slipped out of bed and joined Jerry at the window and looked over his shoulder.

Visible between us and the distant peaks of the Pyrenees was, apart from our garden and fields of vines, absolutely nothing. I had forgotten just how rural this area was and just how close to the edge of town we were. We had neighbours, but from the Juliette balcony of our bedroom, you could only just make out the corners of their gardens. This was a level of privacy we had only dreamt of back in England. Luckily for Jerry!

A few minutes of wistful silence later, Jerry broke the spell and announced he was off for a shower and then to the boulangerie to get us pastries for breakfast and fresh bread for the day. I suggested sharing the shower, but as he pointed out it was less than three hours before the boulangerie closed.

Based on the swearing and screaming from the shower, I was glad I had accepted the rain check on the shared shower. Instead, I started to do a few stretches in front of the open windows. The trouble with cotton is it doesn't give as well as lycra. As a result, after Jerry had dressed and set off to buy our breakfast, I slipped off my nightie and daringly finished my Pilates-inspired stretches, nude. Heaven only knew, at that stage, where my yoga-wear was hidden, put away or awaiting unpacking.

As I showered, I amused myself, stop

it! with the notion that I was also washing my gym kit at the same time. Maybe I would do my stretches bare all the time, after all, only Jerry would ever see me. Besides, my body wasn't in that good a shape that the local youth would gather to watch, and on the other hand, it wasn't that awful I'd scare the horses. I had just finished drying my hair when I heard Jerry coming in.

At least I hoped it was Jerry, I slipped a light robe over my shoulders and tied the belt as I skipped down the stairs. I opened the kitchen door and inhaled the aroma of freshly brewed coffee and croissants. Jerry was just finishing laying everything out on a tray. He looked disappointed.

"I was going to bring breakfast to you, in bed." He sounded and looked like a scolded puppy. Then seeing me glance towards the patio windows, he perked up. "It is very nice out, especially for March, shall we take breakfast outside?"

I nodded and went to open the garden door for him.

Outside we have a couple of terrace areas, offering shade at different times of the day.

Seeing as it was only March, but a warm day for March, it was still cool enough at ten to want to be in the full sun. I dragged the small metal table into position and fetched the chairs, while Jerry laid everything out on the table. Then my darling husband disappeared into the kitchen and emerged with an ice bucket and two glasses. I was a bit disconcerted by this until he produced a half bottle of champagne, non-vintage of course, but the cork popped, the bubbles rushed and we toasted our first breakfast in the sun on our very own terrace. If this was going to be our life in France, bring it on.

We drank champagne and talked all morning under the warm sunlight, as Ray Davies nearly put it in his song Lola, except he is a better poet than me and his version rhymed and more importantly scanned. Oh, and we only sat there until about eleven. Then I went and got dressed and we went shopping for food and drink for the next few days.

I'm a bit of a nerd

That first morning was fabulous, just sitting in the warm sun, Fran looking downright sexy in that silky kimono affair I'd bought her for Valentine's Day a few years' back. As I hoped, it was the portent of days to come, but not yet. The fine sunny stuff held as we went into the city to find the Hypermarché and return via the local *Cave Co-operative*, the town's wine co-operative shop. I was pleasantly surprised that the rain held off while I helped Fran with unloading the car. The rain, however, started to fall as we were putting our purchases away, in The Pantry!

A pantry, for those lucky enough to have been born in the era of refrigerators, freezers, and fitted kitchens, is a room. Normally a small, dark and often damp room on the north side of a house, just off the kitchen. These cool, dark rooms were lined with shelves and were used to store everything for the kitchen. In times gone by, my nan had one in her house, as did my best friend's mum. Both were famous repositories of biscuits, crisp and tins of beans, for young boys!

The pantry in our new house is a thing of great functional beauty. The windowless room is on the cool, north side of the kitchen. The walls lined with shelves, wooden shelves on the east and west facing walls. The ones on the north facing wall are made of marble, the lowest of which sits on a stone plinth and has a shallow basin carved into it. Except, the middle of the basin is a marble-topped island, like a castle surrounded by a moat. Fran didn't get it at first, but I'm a bit of a techno-nerd and soon had it identified. It was a cooling shelf.

'What's a cooling shelf?' I hear you young whippersnappers asking. I'll ignore the word 'Grandad' at the end of the sentence, because I will be soon. A long story, I'll tell you about it later if we get time.

A cooling shelf was a form of pre-electric fridge. You put your carefully wrapped piece of meat, on a plate onto the 'island' in the sink. Then you fill the 'moat' with water and taking a piece of wet muslin, cover the meat with the damp cloth, trailing the material into the water in the moat. As the water evaporated from the muslin, it cooled the air. You do remember from physics? The latent energy of evaporation? The fact that the muslin trails into the water in the 'moat' enables the water lost in evaporation to be replaced by a wicking process; you remember surface tension?

Sorry, I did warn you I was a bit of a techno-nerd, I got a bit carried away there. Suffice to say, properly set up, the cooling shelf 'should' keep your steak fresh enough to last from an early morning shop (when the temperature is still low, sorry techno-nerd again) until you chucked it on the barbie for dinner.

Let's just say I love The Pantry in a way that Fran finds incomprehensible. To her, I think it is just a large, walk-in cupboard, a wardrobe for food. To me, it is a room of treasures, a memory from childhood, a great example of the carbon-free technologies we need to look at with fresh eyes and a great place to keep wine.

Yes, I know, you keep wine in the cellar. I will keep wine in ours too, but on a wet and windy night, or in the middle of an interesting conversation around the dinner table, I'll be damned if I am going outside to unlock the cellar and rummage around in the dust and cobwebs for another bottle of wine. The pantry will house our 'short-line' store, like the 'ready to use locker' where a few rounds of ammunition are kept near a warship's guns. Sorry more nerdish knowledge on display!

As I was saying, the rain arrived as we were putting our purchases away. I had been planning to cut the lawn during the latter part of the day. Again, that is a well, almost. It isn't really a lawn as we would know it in an English garden. What we have, where an English house would have a grass sward, is a selection of less woody weeds, grasses and other plants. It covers almost a thousand square metres of the one-acre plot. The rest is an orchard of assorted trees. I had in mind the creation of a couple of pathways through the savannah grasslands to link up the shed, the pool, the garage and the house leaving the rest as meadow for a while.

Instead, we spent the afternoon sat in one of the sheltered areas of the terrace and, armed only with five kilos of French-English dictionary, set about translating the posters we'd seen at the Cave Co-op. Both Fran and I speak reasonable French, well we get understood even if we can't understand the locals. We struggled however to decode the language of the posters. Fran came up with a solution; she does that from time to time. Using the camera on her phone, she took pictures of the interesting looking ones and we worked on those.

Apart from the ones for forthcoming *Vide Grenier*, translated literally as empty attic and as good a name for a boot fair as any. Fran observed that I might want to check our attic, to see if there was any treasure. I riposted with a barbed comment about '*Vide Armoires*' only to be hit with a counter threat of Fran organising a *'Vide Abri'*. Translated the 'vide armoire' would be an empty wardrobe, and no armoire has anything to do with loving clothes!

On the other hand, as I thought about it, the *Vide Abri* (Empty Shed) was a rather interesting proposition. Imagine having to go out and replace all my old tools and machinery with new stuff. "Sorry sweet, I'd love to prune the apricot tree. Although I have to go to *Brico-Jardin,* our local DIY store (Brico) and garden (Jardin) centre, for a new ladder, secateurs and shredder first! I could go and get them Monday when they reopen."

According to my French Grammar for Beginners, they should be Abri or Armoire Vide, but being French, the word order is reversed for a Vide Grenier. My bank account would get re-ordered too if either of the other suggested Vide events was to happen.

The next poster we managed to translate was for an omelette of some sort, well we knew that before we started. We had even worked out that it was a lunchtime, on a Monday, some three weeks off. It took a while, but we soon understood what it said, if not what it meant. It was some sort of communal lunch with wine, a band and games for children at a fair price. Tickets could be bought at the bar and the boulangerie. I cleverly tied the date to Easter Monday and then identified the word Paques as meaning Easter too. So we had an event, open to all, wine and something to do with an omelette. Researching this called for 'Mr Google'. Off to the bar to get some 'wiffy' and some beer, it would be churlish not to, after all.

I didn't get a beer in the end.

My Husband's a geek

No, Jerry didn't get his beer. I reminded
him we still had to make our supper. I
also reminded my husband that what he
always refers to as 'the bar' is, in fact, a
café, bar, restaurant. Since we had tried
the restaurant and bar parts last night, it
was our turn to try the café today.
Besides, I wasn't going to carry him home
again tonight.

The coffee was good, a bit strong, but
pleasant with a glass of water. The Wi-Fi
worked very well and we discovered all
about the *Lundi de Paques* tradition. It is
an Easter Monday picnic with friends and
family, where you are served an omelette
made with the Easter eggs, the eggs that
the children would hunt for as one of the
'animations'. Locally, it was traditional to
make a wild asparagus omelette, we
discovered to our delight.

That, we decided, was going to be
our introduction to community life. I sent
Jerry to buy two tickets from the bar
owner. It turned out that there were no
real tickets. We were signed up and
Marcel, the bar owner according to Jerry,
had taken the money and our names
were on the list! Ah well, when in France,

I hoped.

Taking another sip of coffee, I logged into my e-mails. There were only about twenty-five today. Most were junk, a few from family members, distant family members, wanting a free holiday. Then I found it and experienced one of those 'only in France' moments.

Our new wi-fi router was being delivered to our the local 'Brico-Jardin' today and our line would be activated before the end of the day. I was stunned, who would send someone an email to tell them that their internet was now available? I mean, if we hadn't come to the bar to get access, how would we ever find out we were online? Still, we were going to have the internet at home by bedtime!

Jerry was quite sanguine about it.

"Just as well I decided against having a beer, isn't it?" He concluded and finished his coffee.

I just stared at him, totally gobsmacked, I believe, is the expression.

"What's up?" He put his cup down. "If I'd had a beer we wouldn't be able to drive to Brico-Jardin. Would we?"

I shook my head; it was less than a quarter of an hour since he was throwing a paddy about me not allowing him to have a beer. Men!

At least we got away from the bar sober and early enough to make it to Brico-Jardin before closing. Once we had sussed out where the customer service desk was, it was a very simple job to collect our parcel. The harder job was getting the child out of the sweetie shop. No, that's unfair to children in confectionery shops. Getting Jerry out of a 'boy's toys' store has always been difficult. It was worse than ever this time. Lots of new toys, some he had never seen before, others had different plugs on to his British versions. It might be better to replace them with ones built for the French electrics and accessories! Fortunately, it was nearly closing time and I found a catalogue of all their best toys.

I thrust the catalogue in his hand, reminded him that he had to set up the wi-fi and then he could do some price comparison research. I jogged his memory about the time he had bought a power washer, only to find it was available at the other DIY superstore in town for little over half the price.

The thought of playing with the wi-fi and then hunting online bargains was too much for him to resist. We left the store with just our parcel and the catalogue. There is a first time for everything.

When we got home, Jerry disappeared into the 'study'. I got on with preparing our evening meal. From time to time there were mutters and mumbles about how strange the connectors were. I ignored them.

A little later, I heard Jerry storming from room to room with his tablet PC muttering, "Good signal here; that's a bit weak; Oh God, no signal in here!" That was rather worrying; it appeared the chap in the phone shop had been right…

While we in placing our order for the phone and the internet, the young man who was looking after us had suggested that we might want to invest in a couple of wi-fi mains range extenders. Jerry had pointedly reminded the young chap that few houses are fifty metres long, so the signal should cover the whole house, no problem. The young assistant articulated something about the walls in an old house, followed by a beautifully executed Gallic shrug. No more was said about it until after we left the shop. Then we had a typical Jerry tirade about people who try to take advantage of foreigners. It lasted about ten minutes until I got him into a café and put a cup of coffee in front of him. After that, it had reduced to a few grumbles and curses.

Now it was going to get worse, unless I acted quickly. Jerry would assume he was going to have to go back to the shop and eat humble pie. I can't think of anything that Jerry hates more than humble pie, apart from bad beer and poor service. Time to intervene, I decided.

As Jerry crashed through the kitchen door, I looked up from the magazine I was thumbing through and in my lightest voice, started to 'witter' as Jerry would call it, if he thought I wasn't listening.

"You know the range extender things the man in the phone shop tried to rip you off over; I saw them at half price in the hypermarché. You were so clever, turning him down at that price!"

Jerry beamed as he went through the other door back to the study. Things went quiet for a while. I finished the cooking, dished up and put the steaming plates of food on the kitchen table. Then I called Jerry to come and open the wine and sat down.

Seconds later, Jerry appeared drying his hands on a towel. He drew the cork from the bottle with a satisfying 'pop', as he poured, there was a rather mellow glugging noise. I waited as he raised the glass, sniffed and exhaled with a nod of his head. He then sipped from his glass, holding it up to the light and turning the glass as he savoured the wine.

"Not bad, not bad at all!" He announced his finding to the world at large. He then tucked into our meal. Halfway through, he put down his knife and fork and announced that we had wi-fi in most rooms, a few were a little 'flaky' and if we were to buy a couple of those range extender doo-dahs we could probably be online at the pool!

Face saved, executive decision to solve a different problem that might, coincidentally, solve a real problem; the one that we were not talking about. Live with a 'Jerry' long enough and that will make perfect sense!

After dinner, is it OK with you if I call

our evening meal 'dinner'? Only Jerry insists that tea is a drink, with jam and bread, as Julie Andrews sang in the Sound of Music, and that supper is something you eat at midnight, after coming home from somewhere and before going to bed. Frankly, I really don't care about such things that much, but well Jerry is 'Jerry'.

So! After our evening meal, call it what you will, we took the rest of the bottle of wine and withdrew to the withdrawing room. No, we didn't! Not even Jerry is quite that conceited. We sloped off to the lounge with the bottle and our computers and played on the internet for a few hours. Jerry spent a lot of time comparing prices of various 'tools' across the web. I noticed he had pages from Brico-Jardin, BricoBargain and BricoMonde open at the same time. I also noticed he was being sensible, for him at least, and had the Amazon website open too.

A little later, it started to get cool in the lounge, so we went to bed. The good news was I didn't have to guide, push, pull or carry Jerry up the stairs this time. While he was in the bathroom, I fitted my new gadget to a picture hook on the landing wall. Then I slipped into the bedroom, turning off all the lights as I went. It was gratifying to hear Jerry's moan about the darkness change to complaints about being dazzled, as the motion-activated light leapt into action.

We read for an hour or so before I fell asleep. An article in 'A Life in France' magazine caught my attention. It was entitled, 'New House, New Horizons, New *Voisins*,' that will be new neighbours to you English speakers. The thought crossed my mind, we'd bought the new house and we hadn't yet met our new neighbours. What if they were difficult? Or noisy? At least we couldn't see them from our windows and they couldn't see us, as far as I could work out. As I fell asleep, I must admit it was worrying me a little.

Brushwhacker Challenge

I must say that I was very impressed with Fran's little purchase. Once I was over the shock of the initial flash-blindness, I could see where I was going in between the bathroom and the bedroom, without needing to fumble around for light switches or the torch. That was going to make life much easier.

Later, while I was being tormented by the creatures of the night, with their scraping, scratching, scuttling and screeching, I got to thinking about how effective a warning device this little light could be. I know Fran says dangerous for me to think, but she's not the one staying awake all night on guard duty. What it meant was that if anything was going to enter our bedroom by coming along the landing it would set the light off and I'd get a warning.

With that settled in my mind, I could now ignore the pack of wild cats that were surrounding the house waiting for us to slip up and let them in. So, despite the absence of the reassuring noise of a police chase, I fell into a deep slumber.

The next thing I knew there was a

bright light shining in my eyes. The wolves had broken in, the little light was shining in warning. I braced myself to defend Fran, grabbing hold of her to prevent her being snatched from the bed and torn to pieces.

"That's nice; I like it when you wake up eager!"

Ah, so it wasn't wolves nor wild cats nor even weasels attacking down the landing. The light was, in reality, sunlight streaming through a gap in the shutters over the windows. Still, it was nice to be appreciated, so I went with Fran's initial idea.

When I got back from the boulangerie, much later than yesterday, Fran had put the coffee on and was laying the table for another breakfast in the sun. It was nice watching her floating about in that light, silky dressing gown again this morning. Suddenly the breeze caused it flap open and it revealed that it was all she was wearing.

I held the croissants in a paper bag; they got slightly crushed. Have I told how attractive, sexy and exciting I find my wife? No? Remind me to tell you sometime!

After breakfast, it was time to get on with some of the gardening. Before it gets too hot! In the shed, I had two new toys, bought in England before we left. One was a big, strong petrol lawnmower, bought to replace the electric hover mower that had served to keep our lawn trimmed in the past. The other new toy was a petrol engine strimmer, again replacing a lighter electric one because we had a much longer fence line to keep trimmed. This one rejoiced in the name of Brushwhacker. I soon found out why!

I got the mower started and off we went, for a few metres. Then I had to stop and untangle the brambles from around the blade. Then off we went again. By lunchtime, I had managed to do an area the size of our old front garden and it had only taken me twice as long. There was a small area, between the house and the pool surprisingly, where the mowing had been easy. The rest of the garden, all three thousand square metres of it, was a no-go area for the mower; rocks, bits of timber, thorn bushes and one, maybe two, old tractors littered the rest.

After lunch, Fran and I decided to explore some of the more remote regions of the garden, to see what was there. It turned out I was wrong about the tractors, but everything else was there.

"All these rocks and bits of tree are going to ruin your mower, you'll have to try to find another way of cutting the weeds so that we can clear the ground."

"No shit, Sherlock!" I thought to myself. Now I might be stupid from time to time, but not even I am stupid enough to say this sort of thing out loud, I am rather attached to my balls and want to keep them where they are! That applies even when Fran is reading from the Ministry of the Blindingly Obvious press release.

"I'll try with the Brushwhacker, at least the nylon cord is meant to break if it hits anything hard."

"Well, make sure you wear safety goggles!" And off she went, hopefully, to prepare dinner for the intrepid gardener. Attractive, sexy and exciting, absolutely; I'll add infuriating, maddening and patronising to the list as well.

I went back to the shed and started to kit myself out. Down the front of my heavy jeans went a pair of thick socks. Next, our son's old shin pads went on my legs while I slipped my rather unfashionable leather jacket over my shirts. I then carried the Brushwhacker, its harness, a pair of stout leather gloves, a visor and a pair of ear defenders out onto the cleared part of the lawn. Now you understand, it's not just my balls I value.

Eventually I worked out how to get everything on, in the right order, and start the mighty Brushwhacker. Put on everything, apart from the gloves and the Brushwhacker. You need your hands free to get the Brushwhacker started and attached to the harness. Then put the gloves on, gun the throttle and walk towards your target.

Five minutes later I had to take it all off again to adjust the cutting cord. Eventually I learnt to recognise the things that were breaking the cord and I could whack-a-way at the weeds for ten minutes at a time before I needed a breather.

An hour and a half later I ran out of petrol. It was a good time to stop anyway, so I took the Brushwhacker back to the shed and gratefully removed most of my protective gear.

The kitchen was free from the aromas of cooking and Fran was conspicuous by her absence. Still, there were several bottles of beer in the fridge, so I took one and sat down at the table. Ah, a note.

"Gone to get some fresh fish for dinner. I tried calling you to see what you wanted but you were ignoring me. F"

Ignoring? I mean I was wearing ear defenders to keep out some of the noise of the Brushwhacker and I was supposed to hear her calling. I grabbed another beer from the fridge and went back to survey the results of my afternoon's labour.

"Not bad," I thought, "If I clear away the cuttings I might be allowed to sit and read my book tonight." I put my gloves back on and dragged the wheelbarrow over to where I had started cutting the weeds.

An hour later, when Fran returned with some pork steaks, (so much for fish!) I had four piles of rubbish near the drive. The biggest was the pile of chopped green stuff. That followed in size by the pile of wood, old tree bits and sawn timber, then rocks and the tractors, which turned out to be an old bike and a few very rusty gardening implements from a bygone age.

Fran was very impressed, until she saw how little of the garden I had actually tackled. However, she accepted my argument that I now had acquired a series of effective techniques and the next few days should see the entire garden cleared.

While she was cooking, I took the car and went and bought some more petrol for the machines. In a moment of inspiration, I also went to Brico-Jardin and bought some more of the line for the Brushwhacker. I nearly bought a cutting blade too. Fortunately, another customer, who was also English, pointed out that I would be using a strimmer because the rocks could damage the blades of the mower, so why was I buying a blade for the strimmer? I saw his point immediately and following his advice I bought a spare spool for the line.

After we had eaten our dinner that evening, I sat down to wind the strimmer line onto the spools. Let me tell you it was not an easy job. Fran managed it much better than I did, she seemed to have the knack of getting the line to go on in a neat spiral. The one I did was all crossing and twists. I have no idea what effect this would have.

I did, however, experience the best night's sleep since we arrived in France. I guess clearing some of the long grass had stopped the wild creatures getting so close to the house.

Dressing for the garden

It was almost the worst night's sleep I've had in months. Jerry passed out within seconds of his head hitting the pillow. Flat on his back, head arched back he snored, and did he snore!

I should have known; he had spent most of the day in the fresh air. He had worked hard physically for most of the afternoon too. Last time he had done either would have been at Twickenham during the England versus Argentina rugby match. Mind you that was as a spectator, not a player. The last time he actually played, he was … well, let's say he was less than half the man he is today, and less than half the age he is now.

The last time he had spent a day working in the garden was when he cut the lawn back last September. The lawn at the old house was well-established and had been cared for over the decades. Unlike the 'lawn' here in France, which looks like it hasn't been touched for decades.

I lay there listening to the old git snoring the pigs home, hoping that he wouldn't do himself any damage. We have health insurance, but I didn't want us to be testing it this early in our new life. Besides, our French wasn't up to a doctor's consultation and we were still trying to get registered with an English-speaking doctor. Our contingency was a dash for the UK to see our old GP and that would be difficult to do if Jerry damaged his back!

Unable to sleep, and with the sunlight starting to create golden streams through the darkness of our bedroom, I decided to get up and make an early start on the day. Besides, it was after seven and I needed a pee.

Downstairs, in the kitchen, I made a cup of coffee and sat by the French windows and watched the early shadows sweep across the patch of lawn that Jerry had cleared. Sitting in the apricot tree, near the shed, was a flock of birds all singing their beaks off. I opened the doors so that I could hear them more clearly. It was already warm, like an English day in late spring, and it was still only late March. The air was full of birdsong and I thought I could hear the buzzing of bees from the blossoming trees in our orchard.

It was so peaceful I decided that I would do my morning stretches outside today. I fetched my yoga mat from indoors and was about to spread it on the terrace when I noticed a sunlit glade between the trees. It was in the area that Jerry had cleared yesterday and it looked like an illustration from a children's story. I tucked the mat under my arm and made my way across the lawn.

The glade was obviously a garden feature from a previous era. The trees had been planted in a circle around it and bore the marks of having been pruned and manipulated to leave the area partially screened but open to the sky. The ground underfoot was almost flat and free from rocks and stones; even the grass was of better quality.

I decided then and there this was going to be the place I did my exercises. The place had a calm, tranquil almost healing vibe about it. Other than the roof of one of the neighbour's houses; I could see nothing, apart from the back of ours, the garden and the sky. A great place for some mindful exercise. I rolled my mat out and was about to go back inside, but instead of going and getting changed, I slipped off my slippers and robe. It was the first time I had ever been naked out of doors. Unless you count that time Jerry and I got slightly drunk and amorous after having a barbeque one summer. Well, all of our neighbours' houses had been in darkness, and I tried hard to be quiet.

My exercise regimen takes about half an hour and I like to finish with a short period of relaxation, lying flat on my mat, trying to clear my mind ready for the day. This morning I lay there looking up into the clear blue sky, listening to the low drone of the bees and the birds singing. As I relaxed, I had a vision of people sitting around a large table, laden with freshly cooked meat, vegetables, salads and fruit. They were dressed in a simple style, but everything was clean and smart. Children played on the lawn around the table while the adults drank wine, talked, laughed and relaxed.

That's why they had created this space an outdoor dining room, open to the heavens but protected from the buffeting winds and the intrusive eyes of others. So that's what it will be again, when it is not being used as my exercise area.

I was back on my feet picking up the mat and my robe when I heard Jerry calling from the kitchen. I turned towards the sound of his voice just in time to see him look through the open French windows.

His jaw dropped open, and stayed hanging loose, as rather than putting my robe back on, I gathered it in my hand, tucked the rolled up mat under my arm and sashayed back across the lawn to the kitchen doors. As I walked towards Jerry, I heard him whimper. I don't associate Jerry with whimpering; I must have made an impression. Time to build on it too, I decided.

"What's the matter, big boy, never seen a naked woman walk across the lawn to you before?" I stood in front of him, arms open waiting for an embrace.

I'm certain I heard another whimper, then an hour later I returned to the verandah after my shower, wrapped in a towel. To find Jerry, still naked after our lovemaking, had made breakfast for us. In the absence of patisserie, he had put out some cereals along with the coffee. I undid my towel and wrapped it around my still wet hair. Why do we do that after a shower and not at the pool or the seaside?

We sat down to eat. I was ravenous

by now. Jerry sat down opposite me, and poured a big bowl of cornflakes, added milk and sugar and tucked in. I couldn't help it; it came to me quite suddenly halfway through a mouthful of muesli. I started to splutter, tried to swallow and it got stuck. I took a mouthful of coffee to try to wash it down. The coffee was still very hot. I was burning my mouth and choking at the same time.

It was lucky that most of the stuff that exploded from my mouth missed Jerry. It is surprising how wide an area a mouthful of coffee and half-chewed muesli can cover when propelled by a partially suppressed fit of giggles.

Five minutes later, it seemed longer at the time, I had recovered enough composure to answer Jerry's entreaties to explain what was wrong. I wiped the tears from my eyes.

"It suddenly occurred to me that it was a good thing you were eating corn flakes, not another type of cereal," I paused and wiped my eyes and stifled another fit of giggles, "Otherwise you could have been Jeremy, the Sugar Puffs' Bare!"

I collapsed into another fit of giggles,

the tears running down my cheeks. It occurred to me, it was a good job I wasn't wearing knickers, as they would never have dried. With that, I started laughing all over again, Jerry, bless his heart, just rolled his eyes, poured himself another cup of coffee and finished his cornflakes; while I kept bursting into new fits of giggles every time I looked up and saw him munching away.

Sugar Puff finally finished his breakfast and cleared the table. I sat nursing a cup of coffee, watching the sky, the trees and the birds, snickering from time to time. Jerry reappeared wearing jeans, a T-shirt and heavy boots. He then added a pair of shin pads, some socks down his trouser front and a leather jacket.

He noticed me watching this extreme dressing.

"Stay out of the way while I am using 'The Mighty Brushwhacker', things tend to fly about a bit!" He explained, "If you could give me a hand with the clearing up after I have cut, it would be useful."

"Girlies have their uses then," I thought as I watched him ambling towards the shed.

I continued to watch as he emerged with a pair of leather gloves, some sort of harness, a visor and some ear defenders. He climbed into most of this gear before returning to shed to bring out the strimmer thingy.

The noise of it starting was unexpectedly loud. Then as he started cutting, I understood all the protective gear and the admonition to stay back. As he swung the business end of the strimmer back and forth the air filled with dust, bits of stone and quite large bits of stick or plant whirled past his head. There was a clatter of something hard, travelling at high velocity, smashing against something else hard and Jerry moved on deeper into the undergrowth.

Leaving Jerry to it, I got on with tidying away breakfast and the last bits from the night before. I was about to put the dishwasher on when I was suddenly aware it had gone quiet outside. I popped out on to the verandah and could see Jerry at the business end of the 'MB', I'd decided that this was indeed something more than a strimmer, and Mighty Brushwhacker was as good a name as any. However, seeing Jerry at the business end of the MB, swearing, scared me half to death. Well, they say when

men are seriously hurt they go very quiet,
suddenly I was worried. No need, a few
seconds later Jerry threw the thing to the
ground and came storming towards the
kitchen.

"Run out of line!" he growled by way
of explanation as he stormed into the
lounge to get the reels we had wound the
night before.

New reel fitted, he fired up the MB
again and started cutting again. Only to
stop and fidget with the business end
again. Start it up and repeat the whole
thing every four or five minutes.

I waved a cup of coffee at him while
he was playing with it for the upmteenth
time. We sat and drank it in silence. I
have learnt not to ask what's wrong and
offer solutions in these situations. The
problem always gets talked through out
loud, if you give it enough room. I poured
a second cup of coffee and finally, it
came out.

"The automatic line feed isn't working.
Every time the line breaks I have to stop
and pull out more line. Even then it is
difficult to get it to unwind from the spool."
Cue, me making some useful
contribution; Oh no! Not this girl; I learnt

that lesson years ago.

"I'm sure if you think about it, you'll find whatever it is that has changed since yesterday. I'll get you some biscuits to help you think." Off I go to the kitchen. You see how clever I have been? I have pointed him at 'changed' and left it to him to work out that it was the spool of string stuff. I bet he used that tangled mess he wound. Meanwhile, I have found the pack of chocolate biscuits he picked off the shelf while we were in the Hypermarché. I have put a few biscuits on the plate, and I'm heading back out to the terrace. As I pass through the french windows a gust of wind pulls my robe apart, using my spare hand I pull the thing shut and continue to the table. I popped the plate onto the table and retied my robe before sitting down.

Two biscuits later, there was a moment of inspiration. Jerry got up and went to fetch the other spool of nylon cord. Knowing that my work was done, I put all the coffee stuff on a tray and picked it up. The robe did its thing as I stood, but with both hands full; I continued to carry the tray into the kitchen rather than put it down, faff around with the tie, and start again. As Jerry passed me, he smiled then commented that the brambles and thorny stuff might get caught on my robe and slow things down in the garden.

I wasn't sure if it was a compliment or not, maybe it was the earlier memory of my very first experience of being bare in the open air had me thinking that way. Either way, I went to get dressed. I found an old pair of jeans and a white T-shirt and slipped them on, along with a pair of sandals that have seen better days. The jeans must have shrunk, I mean I've lost a lot of weight since I bought them, diet, the exercises and a lot of walking, but they felt uncomfortable.My new jeans were fine yesterday, two sizes smaller but they were comfy. This pair must have shrunk in the wash as they felt really constricting today.

I wandered back downstairs and checked the fridge for lunch, plenty of salad. Which was just as well, we had no bread. Mind you, if these jeans were telling me the truth, that was no bad thing.

Just then Jerry called to me for some help. I went to help him with gathering up the debris from where he had been working. The next five minutes revealed several key learning points, as our IT tutor used to say, about my clothing choices. Number one, Jerry's choice of clothing wasn't just because he is a wimp. The thorns and spikes stabbed my hands, my arms and all parts of my upper body. I needed gloves, solid leather gloves. I should have worn something with sleeves to protect my arms and something thicker at the front to protect my boobs from getting punctured. My old potter's smock came to mind. In the shed, in a box marked pots, my mind was suddenly clear. I'll borrow one of Jerry's spare pairs of gloves too, while I'm in there.

As I walked towards the shed, I found myself hauling my jeans up by the belt loops every other step. These jeans weren't too small after all! That was good news. I found the smock just where I thought it was, gloves too. I added a short piece of rope tied around my jeans as a belt; and dressed to impress, went back to work.

We worked steadily for an hour or so before Jerry suggested that I should go and start lunch, while he barrowed the last couple of loads around to the front of the house. I gratefully trotted off towards the kitchen, thinking that it was no wonder he had been so tired last night.

"Make sure the beer is cold!" Jerry

called after me.

Before starting on the salad, I took off the gloves and smock and threw them into the corner of the kitchen. The jeans, home now to burrs, thorns and goodness knows what else, followed very quickly. I washed my hands and went to the fridge, checked the beer, five bottles, all cold. I pulled out the lettuce, tomatoes, cucumber, bell peppers and some fennel for the salad and carried them to the work area. By now I had realised that all was not as it should be with my bra either. I slipped my arms out of the straps turned it around and unhitched it. Looking at it carefully, I could see the bits of bramble, thorn and leaf debris that had managed to inveigle themselves into the inside of my intimate wear, without my consent! Bra added to the pile in the corner, I continued to prep the salad. I was just finishing a dressing, olive oil, raspberry vinegar, garlic, a pinch of mixed herbs, and some finely chopped jalapeno pepper shaken together with a half teaspoon of mustard – my favourite - when Jerry walks into the kitchen.

"Get that gear off, add it to the pile over there," I pointed to my stuff in the corner, "I'll sort it all out after lunch while we relax for a while." I handed him a beer.

A short while later, we were finishing our beer in companionable silence. The salad bowl empty, the ham a memory on the surface of the plates, both of us dressed inT-shirts and pants, boxers for Jerry and rather lacy, black knickers in my case.

"I suppose," I began, "If we are going to finish this garden today, we'd better get on. I'll sort out the gear if you stack the dishwasher."

I gathered up the pile of 'gear' and went out onto the terrace. The boots, gloves, leather jacket and Jerry's harness, I spread out tidily to air a little. The rest I carried up to the line, shook firmly and pegged out each garment. I went and got a brush and was merrily brushing the sticks out of Jerry's jeans when I occurred to me. Not only was I out in the garden but I was also wearing nothing other than a T-shirt and a pair frillies. Ah well, if some man was watching my boobs swinging around under my T-shirt, I hoped they were enjoying the show, because, surprisingly, I was comfy as I was.

We had a second beer each and

looked at the garden with pride. I told Jerry about the clearing and how I had a vision of how it must have been used in the past. He wanted to see where, and how much work was involved, in creating my outdoor dining area. We took our beers and I showed him the place, he poked around a little.

"It could be easily done. There is not much work needed to make it a dining area." I could sense a 'but' coming. "It is a long way from the kitchen and the fridges. Plus, I'm not sure about using a barbeque so close to these trees either. I sort of fancied over between the big fig tree and the fence as a dining area." He pointed to a spot I'd chosen last week. "Besides, I thought you'd like to keep your outdoor gym!" He finished with a smile.

We'll weather the weather ...

I was the first one awake today. After the obligatory first port of call, I headed downstairs. A single glance through the windows, as I put the kettle on, was enough for me to realise I wasn't going to be watching Fran going through her exercises in the garden, let alone doing them naked. I have no idea where she got the idea. In the UK she always, at least when I was looking, exercised in the front room, dressed in Lycra; playing some rather abstract but soothing music all the while. Even clad in Lycra, it was a very entertaining sight from my point of view.

What with all that excitement first thing, then the hard work in the garden, we went to bed very early and to sleep earlier than usual.

While I had slept well, I woke up early and lay in bed with disjointed thoughts running through my head. They managed to coalesce into two concrete actions.

The first was around the trouble I had with the MB (Fran's abbreviation but I'll always steal a good idea). The first and third reels had worked perfectly. It was

only the second that had gone wrong and
failed to unwind because it was tangled.
What I worked out was; my randomly
wound spool caused problems, Fran's
neatly wound one worked. Ergo, I should
get Fran to wind all the replacement
spools of cutting cord. Failing that I need
to learn to wind them more carefully. I
suspected the second option would turn
out to be the way forward.

The second coalesced idea was, that
I must look into getting some Bluetooth
speakers. A pair to put in the trees
around the outdoor gym area to
encourage full and continued use. With a
second pair to put somewhere near the
proposed dining area. I could wire them
up to the main music centre or hook them
up to the phones as the music source.
Amazon here I come!

I took the coffee up to the bedroom
and got mumbled thanks as I put a cup
on Fran's bedside cabinet. I put my coffee
on a chest of drawers before opening the
window shutters. I walked back to my
side of the bed, collecting my coffee en
route.

"It's a bit wet and windy out there
today," I observed as Fran started to sit
up. "I don't suppose you'll be out there for

your exercises this morning!"

I got another mumbled response as she reached for her cup and took a sip and put the cup back down. I took a sip of my coffee while the caffeine was making its way around Fran's system.

"Wet, you say."

"Yep, and windy," I replied.

"Good job we got the garden cleared yesterday, then."

A proper sentence, she was nearly fully functional, another couple of mouthfuls of starting fluid and we will have ignition.

"I'll have my shower while you finish your coffee and think about what you want from the boulangerie." That should give her plenty of time to wake up fully. I threw back the covers and paddled off to have my shower. Two verses of 'Onward Christian Soldiers' I returned to find Fran sat up in the bed, reading emails on her tablet.

"A chocolate croissant would be good and don't forget to get some bread." Fran paused her email reading to put in her breakfast order. "Oh! Denise wants to bring the kids to stay at half term, we will need to get the guest rooms and the pool sorted out."

"Last week in May? That gives us just eight weeks. I'd better get breakfast quickly then!" I was out of the bedroom before the pillow hit the door behind me.

I had an interesting exchange with 'Madam' at the boulangerie. I won't call it a conversation, but it was close. It can only be because we are getting to be regular customers. She had gabbled at me as usual. This time I caught enough words to realise she was gabbling about the weather. I said that if the sun shone every day the vines would have no water and there would be no wine. I would type the words in French to show off how good I am at it, but I struggle with written English, let alone French! Madam obviously thought it was enough to promote me to the status of a friend as she used 'tu' to wish me a good day!

When I carried my recently purchased goodies into the kitchen a few minutes later, Fran was just putting on the coffee machine for the breakfast cuppa. I missed my morning mug of tea, but add a splash of the French milk and it just didn't taste right. It was fine for the coffee but tea, no way.

We sat by the French windows and looked out across the garden, while we ate our breakfast. Fran looked radiant, as always does after a successful work out. She must have been about to shower when I had got back from the boulangerie. I noticed she was wearing very little under her dressing gown.

While she went to have her shower, and do whatever it is that a woman does for an hour in the bathroom, I booted up my computer. By the time she came back downstairs, I had two sets of waterproof, battery-powered Bluetooth speakers on their way from the Rainforest and was browsing for new books to put on my trusty Kindle.

Fran poured us both a cup of coffee, approved of my morning's activities and gave me my list of jobs to be jobbed by dinner time. Most involved the bedrooms, that today were filled with boxes, assorted bits of bed and chests of drawers that in eight weeks would be freshly painted replicas of something out of Country Living.

All day we moved empty boxes to the

shed, emptied full ones and repacked them ready to go into the *'grenier'* to await the time they will be needed or 'vided'. Beyond the Christmas lights and my collection of guitar magazines, I didn't reckon any of it would be of any use, apart from as loft insulation.

That evening we relaxed, glowing with achievement. The two bedrooms were clear of boxes. The furniture was stacked neatly on the landing. Tomorrow I'd go to Brico-Jardin and buy the selected paint and all the brushes.

The days passed. We decorated, we tidied the garden, we ate and drank, and we laughed together and made love.

Meeting the locals

The days passed, I kept on cajoling and nudging Jerry to get on with the tasks in hand. I admit he was doing an excellent job. The walls of the bedrooms were a beautiful, even white. The window panes were free from paint after he finished the frames. They, along with the doors, architrave and skirting were finished in gentle shades of green that complemented the olive green painted shutters on the windows. The beds had been re-assembled, the drawers, wardrobes and dressing tables cleaned, repainted and moved into position by the time Easter arrived.

The *Fete de Paques* was to be our first sojourn into the life of our new community. I was unsure of the protocol for this type of thing, so I packed two hampers. One hamper contained just the hardware, two of each; sets of cutlery, dinner plates, side plates, dessert dishes, wine glasses, water glasses and a corkscrew. The other larger hamper contained all the aforementioned items plus a generous picnic. I wasn't sure just how much food there would be, or if it would pass the quality threshold, and Jerry needs food if he is having a glass or two. The wine was Jerry's task. He decided on taking a litre of the red from the local *cave*, then very sensibly added a bottle of water. Sometimes I am very proud of him.

As it turned out, we only needed the small hamper. The omelette was excellent, served with lots of bread and some salad. There was even a simple dessert of some sort of cake and cheese. Much to Jerry's delight, the wine was delivered to the tables in pitchers red, white and a rather nice rosé, shame I had volunteered to drive. The people around us on the long table were mainly French. We struggled to get involved in the conversation, but they were all wonderfully polite to us and we now knew about a dozen people well enough to be able to greet them by name next time we saw them in town or at Brico-Jardin.

The other long table seated a group of English speakers. Most were immigrants from the UK, some of the others had distinct accents. One voice was louder than the others and seemed to dip, volubly, into the various conversations going on around him.

"Connez-vous Monsieur Roger?" Monsieur Chaubert, one of our new friends, asked. We shook our heads.

Moments later Monsieur Chaubert was introducing the 'new arrivals from England' to Roger Smithson.

"Enchanté Fran; Jerry, call me Roger; I can't abide all this Monsieur and Madame and 'vous' nonsense, we are all 'tu' in our little group!"

Thus, we met Roger, the universally recognised voice of the international community that lived in and around Les Lilas. Whether the rest of the community agreed with him or not, it was his voice you heard.

During the course of the increasingly boozy afternoon, we were introduced to the rest of the anglophones. They were a mix of nationalities: Irish, Canadian, a couple of Kiwis, honorary anglophones from Germany and Holland and of course refugees from all over the UK. Lots of them offered us cards with phone numbers, email and postal addresses with promises of invitations for an 'apero' sometime. We decided we'd have to get some cards printed off too, as we searched for pieces of paper on which to write our contact details.

Roger took one look at our address and said, except being Roger, he announced, "So you are the people who have moved in next to the nudists!" We looked at him amazed. "Oh, yes! They are away at the moment, but your neighbours, I have been reliably informed, are nudist! That will be fun for you in the summer if they come back."

I managed to drag Jerry away, while he was still capable of walking, with promises of meat, an almost raw steak, always a good way of getting him home from buffets and picnics. Jerry is one of those men for whom a meal is just a snack without meat.

While we were eating and enjoying a glass of water, we chatted about the people we had met. We kept coming back to our nudist neighbours. We hadn't seen the neighbours on one side. We had been told, by the immobile Mme Slade, that we had German owners one side and a British couple, who had shouted a friendly 'Bonjour' when we came to view our house for the first time, on the other. The Germans, it had to be the Germans, after all, they go naked in parks and they just drop their shorts when they change on the beach! Ah well, they were away and besides, we could only see a few metres of their garden from upstairs, so no problem. Unless, some of their nudist orgies got too wild, but we'd cross that bridge when we got there. After all, Roger had seemed to doubt they would be around this summer.

"It could be they had trouble with the Marie or the police in the past. That would explain how Roger knows about them and why they might not be back." Jerry suggested.

I supposed we'd find out all in good time. Besides, if these nudists were like Sylvia, one of the nurses I worked with at the hospital, they wouldn't be into noisy sex parties. I knew for certain she was a naturist, she'd told me herself.

The days continued to pass as I sorted out the soft furnishing for the bedrooms, tidied the rest of the house and got ready for Denise and the grandchildren. While I was sorting inside, Jerry was tidying the garden and the outside areas.

During those few weeks, he had managed to paint all of the ground floor window shutters and the ones on our bedroom balcony. The improving weather had enabled him to mow the grass area several times, the area of my outdoor gym was now cut nicely and rolled smooth. With a little bit of watering, the grass there would do well all summer. He had sorted out the outdoor dining area, levelling the table and removing all the debris that might cause people to trip and chairs to tip. The cover was off the pool and it looked ready to go.

Pool maintenance 101

I just read that last bit, about the cover and 'the pool being ready to go'. It rather understates the amount of work involved. After the cover was pulled back, I was faced with a half-full pool, thick with algae, littered with dead leaves and the bodies of creatures great and small. OK, make that creatures 'small and tiny'.

I spent days scooping the muck out of the pool. Then there were the hours of bucketing more water out to lower the water level a bit more. After that, I went around, in my fishing waders, with the pressure washer to clean the waterline staining. On to the chemicals.

To start the chemical treatment, I had to fill the pool back up a bit so that the pump could circulate the water then add a kilo of chlorine powder. I ran the pump for a day, cleaned the filter, added more chlorine and turned the pump back on, while water from the hosepipe slowly raised the water level until the pool was full.

No, we are not finished yet!

At that point, I had to adjust the pH of

the water until it was in the correct range. Then the anti-algae stuff had to be added, followed by another high dose of chlorine! All the time, skimming the leaves and insects off the surface, vacuuming the bottom of the pool, monitoring the levels of the chemicals and keeping the filter system clean.

As you can see, there was a fair bit of work between the cover coming off and 'the pool being ready to go'. In fact, according to what I was reading on the interweb, there is work to do most days until the cover goes back over the pool in October! Still, the water is reaching what we called 'warm' for the old school pool before we turned into softies. It would be plenty warm enough for the grandchildren, based on our last visit to the English seaside with them!

Keeping my man

Yes, Jerry had the pool well under control and the garden was coming along nicely. With the end of our tasks in sight, I decided to let him have a little bit of time off the leash and we went out for lunch at the bar.

The menu de jour always looked rather splendid and amazing value, whenever I had noticed what was on it. Today it offered a 'salade composé' a mixed salad with ham, eggs etc. Followed by coq au vin, with a patisserie of the day for dessert. Served with a quarter litre of wine for a princely €12.90. Stunning value for money I thought, and it was all going well, until Jerry slipped inside to go to the loo.

Ten minutes later, I had finished the last of the wine and he still wasn't back. I went to look for him, it didn't take long to find him. He was stood at the bar with another pichet of wine, deep in conversation with our host about the *Fete de Printemps*, the spring fair, that was upcoming in a couple of weeks' time. There would be some sheep, a few stalls selling local produce and tractor demonstrations by day, then in the evening, wine, food, more wine, music and dancing. The big draw, the reason Jerry was being courted, was the tug-o'-war contest against the surrounding communes.

Men of Jerry's build are not common in our part of France. When he played rugby, he had been a little on the slight side to be a good second row forward. Nowadays, he had the build of a very solid member of the scrum, if not the musculature.

Having lost all three of the round-robin pulls last year, Marcel, the team manager, as well as the bar owner, was trying to add weight to his team to avoid another humiliation. As far as Jerry was concerned, this was his in, his chance to become part of the community. I suppose I was, stupidly, rather pleased for him.

The training schedule had him out of the house three evenings a week for a couple of hours. There would, of course, be the obligatory debriefing over a verre or two after each session, team building, he said.

It turned out that being in the tug-o'-war team was not having the benefits for Jerry that I had hoped for. By the end of the first week, I could see the changes in him. He'd put on a kilo or so in weight. His eyes had developed a yellowish tinge. I also noticed we were getting low on paracetamol. Time to intervene, I decided, as I emailed Denise to ask her to pop into Mega-Drug and buy a few packets of cheap paracetamol to bring out. They are one of the things that are much less expensive in England than in France.

I had been regaled the names of his team mates and the tales of their daring deeds on a number of occasions. Enough, that when I was introduced to one of the other 'Wags' in the boulangerie, we could compare notes. From there on we made a plan.

The team would need cheer-leaders, we, The Wags, would be the thing that could make a difference, so while the boys were pulling an old tractor up and down the car park outside the 'Salle des Fetes', as the village hall was known, we were inside practising our cheers. Not that we were any good, our best one was all shouting P - U – L – L! Pull! while sticking our bums out and jumping backwards. It was my brilliant suggestion to do it in English so the other teams wouldn't know what we were shouting!

Still, I got to know some of the girls really well and we enjoyed our debriefing sessions in the bar, more than the boys seemed too.

The last week of training was rather disrupted by the arrival on the Saturday before the fete by Denise and the grandchildren. After a day of playing football, swimming and computer games with James and Henry, we were both rather tired. No, I'll be honest, we were shattered! The rest of the teams continued to train hard, as we tried to catch enough sleep before the terrible twosome struck again.

Local Heroes

The morning of the fete was hectic. I had additional duties after the regular round of tidying and cleaning up of the pool. I managed to get most of it done before breakfast, a late breakfast but I got it done. Then it was off to the bar, no not for an early snifter, it was HQ for the work party.

OK, so we started with a quick one before getting the tables out of the Marie – one of those wonderful French innovations, the Town Halls all have tables and chairs available for local use, free! As I was saying, we had to get the tables out and arrange them around the square ready for the stall holders. More tables and chairs were stacked up outside the village hall. From there, they would either be arranged in the main hall or the courtyard outside, depending on the weather. Meanwhile, the technical team were generating whistles and howls from the PA system they were trying set up.

By mid-morning, the stallholders and displays had started to arrive and get set up for the official opening at 11:30. The mayor was to give a short speech of welcome. After that, 'Miss Spring' was supposed to drive a flock of lambs across the square. I say was supposed, because there wasn't going to be any participation from 'Miss Spring' this year. The only entrant for this year's pageant, a skinny sixteen-year-old had been disqualified. Not so much for being a boy, I gather it had more to do with the nature of the bribes offered and threats issued to ensure that he would be the only contestant and therefore the first male winner of the title, which had upset the committee.

Fran, Denise and the boys arrived just as the square started to fill with residents and strangers, all anxious to avoid the mayor's speech but be on time for lunch! As it happened, the boys in the technical team had done a great job. The PA system died as the mayor started to speak and returned in time for him to declare lunch open.

Lunch, a plate of lamb and potatoes served with a carafe of local wine was accompanied by much singing. Initially led by a choir of shepherds, it degenerated into the sort of thing that only occurs in England, post-match, in rugby clubhouses. We soon found ourselves trying to out-sing the tug-o'-war teams from the other villages.

I think that ended up as a four-way draw.

As host village, we had the honour of being involved in the first 'Pull' against last year's winners. No contest it turned out, their anchor man was still finishing his (third) lamb steak as we received the call to the rope. As he picked the rope up, the lamb fat on his hands must have coated the rope. One-nil to us. The second pull was much harder, lasting nearly two minutes before the sight of our cheers leaders getting ready to do their stuff, gave us an extra burst of energy. First-round two-nil, and a big psychological advantage over the other teams. We could tell from the amount of wine they were imbibing!

During the next contest, while our defeated opponents were partaking of a consolatory cup of red and another lamb steak, our cheerleaders kept us supplied with water! The next round saw us convincingly pulling a much lighter team from 'Les-Bains' without much difficulty.

The other second-round pairing saw last year's winners lose two ends to one against the team from Villeneuve-la-Lac.

There was much celebration after that result. Villeneuve had lost the contest by the same margin the year before, and with it the championship.

There was a short break between the end of the second round and the last one while the arena was used for a sheep-shearing demonstration that involved two local champions trying to match a man in an ornate collar, the Master of the Pyrenees, or some such hero.

During the break, despite the best efforts of our manager, Marcel, to break the blockade, the cheerleaders kept us away from the drink. From the noise we could hear from the distant corner of the field, 'Team Villeneuve' were already celebrating their victory over the Les Lilas pansies. Last year apparently, we were pulled in less than fifteen seconds, twice!

First, the two double looser teams pulled against each other for the wooden spoon. All three ends were dire contests. In the end, last year's champions salvaged some honour and finished third. Then we were on.

The first end went against us while we were in the ascendency. Stepping back as we pulled Villeneuve towards the mark, the chaps at three and four on our side had lost their footing, tangled with each other and gone down. We didn't make that mistake in the second pull and smoothly eased our way back until the flag was across the mark. One end each, it was all on the third.

Our opponents suddenly knew they were in a fight. This time there was no laughter during their preparation for the pull. Dark words were shared, along with a flask of something inspirational. The umpire called us to the rope.

The pull was evenly balanced for nearly a minute before Les Lilas deployed their trump card. Suddenly our cheerleaders were alongside us, chanting P-U-L-L Pull and jumping back. It seemed to help we took a few centimetres off them. P-U-L-L Pull and the girls jumped again, a few more centimetres. A third chorus P-U-L-L Pull a jump and suddenly we were flying backwards. We had won!

The team from Villeneuve were on the ground laughing and pointing. I followed their line of sight, just in time to see Pascalle pulling up a pair of peach coloured panties and smoothing down her short skirt.

When our captain and Pascalle's
husband, Jean-Luc, was presented with
the trophy, the mayor also called Pascalle
up and presented her with a bunch of
flowers for her contribution to the victory!
After that, the party began in earnest.
There was much singing and the wine
flowed. There was a meal, (I know
because I found the evidence on my
shirt!) a band, dancing and more wine. At
some stage, Denise had taken the boys
home. It was much later that L'Ancre (the
Anchor) and the Chef de Chorus found
our way back to bed.

The following morning, I 'sort of'
came round in bed. I had vague
memories of the celebration party.
Several bottles of wine, some loud music
and I think there was some food. I also
had an image of Margaret dancing on the
table and deciding to finish with a dive
into her husband's arms … and missing.
It was all OK though; the floor caught her!
I think we walked home soon afterwards.
I'll have to check with Fran when she
wakes up.

I eventually prised my eyes open
again. I had to. I was supposed to be
taking Denise and the boys to the airport
in time for their early afternoon flight back
to the UK. As I staggered from the bed,

my thighs stiff as steel bands from yesterday's exertion, I could hear the boys hurtling downstairs towards the pool for their last, first dip of the day. Perhaps someone would think to put the kettle on for the coffee I desperately needed. On the landing, I collided with our daughter as she tagged along behind her sons.

"I'll make coffee for you two! I expect you both need one after last night!" The look of disgust on her face suggested we had let her down. "How many times did you tell Gavin and me about being careful and not getting drunk when we went out and look at you! As for Margaret and the finale to her table dance..."

"Oh, that really happened then!"

"Yes Dad, and put some clothes on before you come down!"

Ah, clothes! They must be in the bedroom somewhere, I guessed. Meanwhile, I had to get to the bathroom.

Relieved, I went downstairs with a towel wrapped around my waist to get the coffee. I didn't dare run the risk of waking Fran without a cup of coffee to thrust at her! Denise just tutted at me as I picked up the mugs with shaking hands.

"Did you enjoy the fete?" I asked trying to deflect her disapproving eyes from the spill she was expecting to happen at any second.

"It was rather good fun, but I just hope the boys can't remember all the words to the song you were trying to teach them! They sang it all the way home last night and I'm guessing that the words are rather rude from the way you and Mum were giggling about them!"

Ah! Time to make a tactical retreat. I took the coffee upstairs, where Fran was starting to groan.

The neighbours part 1

We got back from the airport, both of us tired, hungry and thirsty after having eaten only a very light breakfast. As we were getting out of the car, we heard the sounds of movement from next door. I'm as sociable as the next person, but coffee and something a little 'morish' was called for, before anything else. We had the kettle on boiling and were munching chockie biscuits, when the doorbell rang.

"Hello, neighbours!" I was greeted as I opened the front door. The couple on the doorstep looked like they had enjoyed a sober sleep the night before. They were holding out a bottle of wine and what looked like a packet of English sausages!

I accepted the sausages and managed to say something that must have sounded like 'come in' because they stepped past me into the house. They must have been into the house before as they headed straight to the kitchen. Jerry was sat at the table, looking rather blankly at our visitors.

"The fete, yesterday, tug-o'-war. We won!" I explained.

"I gathered, we heard the news as soon as we arrived in town!" The woman laughed, took back the sausages, found the frying pan and lit the gas. Meanwhile, the chap had located the coffee and a fresh jug of life was underway.

"I'm guessing here, but I'd say we are in the company of L'Ancre and the Le Chef." He nodded towards Jerry.

Say what you want about English sausages but as a post-alcoholic restorative, I have yet to find better. Jerry, bless him, got himself restarted and found the bread, butter and Dijon mustard for the sausage rolls.

Less than an hour later, we were recovered enough to show our neighbours, Ian and Christine, around the house, showing off what we had achieved so far.

After the tour, Jerry did something either very brave or totally foolhardy. He opened a bottle of wine for us to toast being good neighbours. We took the glasses out into the garden. The neighbours were impressed by what Jerry had managed to get done in such a short time.

That lasted until we reached the pool. Jerry had been on about how he had been struggling with the water's condition since mid-week. I hadn't been in for a couple of days, what with the cheerleader rehearsals and stuff. I was horrified to see it was so murky, not that it had gone green, it was just cloudy. Jerry was mortified and mumbled something about how it had sparkled just a few days earlier.

"I expect it is just gunk from the kids' feet and costumes!" Ian was refreshingly upbeat. "Just give it a good shock with the chemicals at sunset and leave the pump running overnight. That'll sort it! It happens to nearly everyone, especially when they have family to visit!"

"It even happened to us!" Christine laughed, but I caught her murmuring "Just the once", under her breath.

We finished the bottle between the four of us. I discovered that Christine, "Call me Teen. There were three of us in my class at school, Big Chris, Little Chris and me. I hated being called 'Chris-three', so I took the other end of the name!" has a great sense of humour.

I was in bed when Jerry came in from

his final check of the pool. "It looks a lot better already", He chimed.

"They seem to be a nice couple." His t-shirt flew into the corner near the laundry basket. "The advice about the pool appears to be spot on." His trousers hit the basket and fell on the floor. "Yes!! Basket!" He air-punched as his underpants caught on the edge of the basket and hung there.

"Yes, they do seem to be nice people, which is just as well, remember we have the other neighbours still to meet."

"Oh, yes! The ones that Roger warned us about, and that we would be unlikely to see, you mean?"

"Yes, those ones, so it is just as well that Ian and Teen are such nice people. Pick up your clothes when you come back from the bathroom. I'm going to try to catch up on my sleep." I turned off my bedside light and snuggled down into the quilt.

Return of the Inner Nerd

By the time I got back from the bathroom, Fran was purring, as she insists I call her snoring. Like she doesn't sweat, she glows. And, she never, ever, criticises, just makes helpful observations.

As I say, she was already dead to the world. Being honest I was rather glad, my head still felt a little unclear, my stomach was unhappy and my legs were still crippled from yesterday's exertion. I was more than ready for a little shut-eye myself.

I slipped into the bed, shut my eyes and the phone rang! I was suddenly aware that the sun was streaming into the room. I soon discovered it wasn't the phone ringing, it was the alarm, which we had sensibly set for the previous morning coming back around again! Mind you, the ten hours sleep had done wonders for me.

I reached out for Fran. She wasn't there. I look in the other direction, Ah, coffee! Fran must be up already. The cup is cool to the touch; she has been up a while. That would explain the shutters being open too.

The coffee wasn't too cold, so I lay back on the pillows and relaxed again. My thoughts wandered back and forth; the visit from Denise, how much the boys had grown even in the three months since we last saw them, the events of the fete. Ah yes, the events of the fete, the victory celebration, the wine, the singing, the wine, the dancing, the wine, Margaret flying, the wine...

Had I, in all honesty, been safe to drive the family to the airport yesterday? Maybe I need to think about the when's and where's of drinking as well as the how much. A little moderation on days when I need to drive the following day would be in order!

One cup of coffee, one resolution, I wonder if another cup would help with world poverty. I decided not, but I'd go and get a fresh cup and see what happened. I climbed out of bed and descended to the kitchen. The coffee pot was full and hot. I poured a fresh cup. Seeing that the back door was open, I wandered outside. It was warm in the sunshine. I could hear Fran's music coming from the garden, she must be doing her exercises. If I had some clothes on I'd go and watch!

Oh, sod it! I'll go dressed as I am, I expect nobody will see me if I'm careful, especially not my lovely wife! I mean it is a joy to watch her, but she sometimes gets a tad upset about me lurking around her. Holding my cup in my hand, I set off in the direction of the exercise area. Walking casually, quietly, but oh so carefully.

"Jerry!" Damn, I've been spotted, I'll just have to brazen this out!

"Hi, love! Thanks for making the coffee!" I wave the cup to show I have one. "Just on my way to check on the pool, I wondered if you wanted to have a look too?"

"I've just finished and was on my way to the shower. I'll look later."

Well, that had gone rather well, Fran hadn't even commented on my lack of clothes! Mind you she was not in any position to comment. She hadn't got her robe with her either. Not that she needs it as far as I am concerned, her exercise regime has made her look pretty buff in the buff! I'm not sure it was such a good idea to try to sneak up on her without preparing. Now I must go and look at the pool, and walk back without clothes.

The pool looks great when I get there, the water has regained its sparkle. Apart from a few leaves and insects which I'll fish out, it's perfect. I grab the net and start to scoop up the blow-ins. It is one of those satisfying little tasks, so many different ways to reach the objective, like playing with a desktop executive toy. I started humming my pool cleaning ditty, Winnie the Pooh would be proud to have made it up. It is almost as good as "The more it snows, tiddly pom!"

> "Skimming high, dipping low.
> Sometimes fast, sometimes slow
> Catch the leaves before they ..."

"Hi, Jerry", my Pooh Corner reminisces suddenly vanished. I clutched the net close and looked around. "Jerry?" It was Fran! Relief swept the adrenaline from my body. "Breakfast is ready, come and get it!"

"On my way!" I called back. Putting the net down, I picked up my empty cup and walked back towards the house. Fran was fresh out of the shower. Her towel draped over her chair as she threw one of the spare pool towels over my chair and gestured me to sit. Coffee, milk, cereals, yoghurt, fruit and orange juice, everything was on the table. No way to slip in and grab a dressing gown on the pretext of fetching something. It was going to be breakfast, naked in the garden. At least I had the better view!

After we had eaten, I made my excuses and slipped off to have my shower and to get dressed. It was going to be a warm day, according to the on-line forecast, something approaching the 'Phew Wot a Scorcher' headline of the British tabloid newspapers. As a result, I kept it light, a short-sleeved shirt and a pair of baggie shorts. Being fashion conscious, I slipped on a pair of those funny little sock things under my trainers.

Properly attired, I returned to the empty kitchen. The washing up was piled high in the sink and the coffee machine was just starting to make those 'I'm finished' gurgles. Fran had not waited long before disappearing if the filter machine was still running. Stopping in passing to grab another cup of my favourite pick-me-up, I went in search of my favourite lady. I found her very quickly, by the simple expedient of following her voice.

When I first saw her, I thought she had flipped! She had moved one of the pool chairs and was sitting on it, a cup of coffee in hand, talking to herself. As I got closer, she saw me and gave a little wave. Then I heard her saying, "Jerry is just coming, I'll have a chat with him and let you know!" Then I understood when I heard Teen's voice coming through from the other side of the hedge that separates the two gardens.

"Right-o! I'll catch up with you later!"

"What was all that about?" I enquired as I got closer to my, totally sane after all, wife.

"Teen was inviting us over for an apero at theirs this afternoon, a reciprocal snoop around sort of thing. Ian is doing their pool this morning," She finished.

I listened hard, but I could hear no sounds. I commented to Fran about it while agreeing to the plan.

"Ah, that's because you are not at the 'talking place' so you can't hear anything." Seeing my bewildered look, Fran went on to explain, "Most of the hedge is very effective at stopping all but the loudest noises from either side being overheard.However, there is a short stretch, where Teen and I were sitting that the sound carries through really well.

Teen thinks it is to do with their shed acting as some form of directional amplifier. I have no idea what she means, but it works!"

That tripped off my inner nerd again! I remembered reading about the big sound location walls they had built in the First World War and again, just before the Second, to detect incoming aircraft. Could it be something like that? Combined with projection acoustics, like the Hollywood Bowl, for projecting sound? Explaining that was the death knell for the conversation. Fran went off to get into some clothes. I went and fished a couple of butterflies out of the pool; while I contemplated the shaped required for the 'talking place'.

Having decided that the same curved surface would focus the sound both ways, albeit inefficiently, I shambled back to the house. My mind, now clear of diagrams of reflection paths, detected a change in the light. It was starting to cloud over a little and some of the clouds looked impressively tall. 'That'll be to do with hot, humid air rising quickly into the unstable air above,' I quickly analysed the atmospheric conditions, 'Thunderstorms before long!'

"What?" I didn't realise I had been talking out loud, Fran had heard my muttering.

"I was just pontificating about the chance of thunderstorms in a little while, my darling." I pointed to the gathering clouds to the south and west of us, just as a smaller example of the clouds obscured the sun.

"That'll be sad, Teen was suggesting we had our drinks and snacks by the pool. Looks like it will have to be an indoor event, assuming your weather prediction is correct." Just as Fran was finishing her thought, my phone pinged, a text message. It was from our telecom provider.

"There are warnings of oranges, no, an orange warning of *orages,* Thunderstorms, in our area. Please take precautions to protect your equipment," I translated out loud. "There is a web link too."

"Protect our equipment? What do they mean?" A chance for the inner nerd to shine.

"I think that they are suggesting that we disconnect all the computer equipment from the mains along with the telephone line and that we unplug the TV too," I explained to an obviously underwhelmed Fran.

Taking a hint from the disparaging look on Fran's face I went indoors and got on with the unplugging. "Would you like me to tether your laptop to your mobile so you can use the 4G?" I called out. The reply was about tethering something else, and I happily went along with that. Mr Grey has had an impact, way beyond colour charts!

Getting to know me

Jerry was right about the weather, an hour or so of thunder, followed by intermittent heavy showers. The apero was indoors rather than, as Teen and I had planned, by the pool. It didn't stop Teen from laying out a fantastic display of snacks that my husband spent the afternoon scarfing down! We looked around their house, Ian and Teen might have owned the place for years, but you could tell they were summer-only visitors.

The upstairs rooms, apart from the master bedroom, felt damp and unopened, with the beds left covered and dust on the mirrors. The views from the windows revealed a much smaller garden than ours. The vista was open across the fields and distant mountains to the south at the bottom like ours, but lined at both sides by solid hedges. The angles were such that you couldn't see into our garden.

This year they weren't expecting to be able to spend much of the summer in Les Lilas. The plan had been for them to be in the USA. Ian was pencilled in to do some contract work for a friend's business. It was all a bit of a con, Ian was to charge his friend's company a fortune for doing it. While basically, Ian and Teen would be enjoying an all expenses paid holiday. After the final report was written-up, the companies owner would fly over and have a series of meetings about the implementation strategy.

Obviously, it was to have been an all expenses paid holiday in France for the friend and his wife. The spending money having already been taken out of the company and paid into Ian's bank account.

"But it's all gone pear-shaped, the software supplier, who was to have written the new system got bought out. Without a system to install, my project can't happen. The good news is that we are here for the summer and our American friends will be over to commission me in a few weeks, well they'll be here for a week's visit." Ian picked up his glass and toasted, "Summer in the South of France."

It seemed a pleasant toast to us, so we joined him. Later I asked Teen how she felt about fiddling the taxman like that. She explained that she wasn't morally concerned. After all, it was the American taxman and all they seemed to do was buy military stuff with it.

A little while later, the weather improved slightly, the clouds broke up and the sun made a valiant effort to shine between the showers. We took our drinks outside and had a quick look around the well-screened garden. The smaller area meant that they had been able to better manage the planting and landscaping than we had. There were neatly laid out pathways leading from the house to the building I guessed was the sound-focusing shed, another led towards the bottom of the garden, passing the washing line and ending near a gate in the fence. A third path led from the shed past the pool area to join the other path so you could approach the pool from either side.

The pool area was security fenced, in accordance with French law, but the fence was now completely hidden under a scrambling mass of roses, jasmine, honeysuckle and passion flower that had grown up, over and along the fence. The pool was surrounded by a carefully built white stone patio.

"When we bought the house the pool area surrounds were much darker coloured stone. We changed it after we had burnt our feet a few times!" Ian commented as I wondered about the practicalities of keeping white limestone stain free. I could see Jerry getting upset as he looked deep into the crystal-clear water of the pool.

"Don't get too depressed about it Jerry!" Ian put a consolatory hand on my husband's shoulder. "I have been working at this for a few years now and we haven't had a pool full of children like you had the other day!"

"Be honest with poor Jerry! Nobody has been in the pool yet!" Teen gave Ian a playful shove. "It's still full of chemicals at the moment, we are going to have our first dip tomorrow, if the water warms up a little after all that rain!"

"I can't get the water to stay like this. It keeps going that murky white colour every few weeks!" muttered Jerry, disconsolately.

"That is probably caused by detergents, soaps, deodorants and suntan lotion getting in the water," Ian explained. "You need to make sure people avoid using these products, or shower before they get in the pool."

"What about the risk of getting sunburnt while in the water?" I asked.

"Oh, we have found some sunscreens that bind almost permanently to the skin, they seem to help," Teen explained. "As for the deodorants, do you need one around the pool? Just rinse it off!"

"The real problem is the soapy residues from fabrics. By that I mean things like fabric-conditioners which are meant to stay in clothes after washing. They bind oils and stuff into suspension, causing the cloudy water." I could see Jerry's inner nerd becoming engaged with the science.

"How can we best stop that happening?" You can't fault Jerry on the path of a scientific answer.

"The easy answer is to not allow fabrics into the water!" Ian stated bluntly. "Otherwise, well make sure things are washed and well rinsed in plain water, and minimise the amount of clothing involved. Nothing is best, but Speedo's are better than board shorts which are better than baggies."

Jerry nodded in agreement with the

advice. I thought I caught Teen smiling at something as I replied, "I'll have to stop wearing a bikini top then!" Not that I have, most of the time, for years.

We wandered on around the garden, Teen pointing out the odd plant here and there. When we got to the bottom of their carefully tended plot, Ian opened the gate. Beyond it stood row after row of vines.

"This used to be part of our garden, theoretically I suppose it still is ours. We rent it to Henri for a case of wine a year." There was a considerable chunk of land out there between our fence and the river bed.

Ian went on to explain that they had wanted the winegrower to stop spraying. The Frenchman had also wanted to make changes, so they had struck a deal. Teen and Ian would lease the wine grower the half-hectare at a tiny rental to compensate him for the extra costs of switching to organic growing.

It was reassuring to hear that the vines around our home were farmed ecologically and that we wouldn't be poisoned by spraying all summer. While we were looking at the rapidly sprouting vines, Jerry noticed the gate in the hedge that marked the boundary of our garden.

"Is that a real gate?" Jerry succeeded in demonstrating once again that asking really stupid questions, you can get a lot back by way of answers.

"Didn't your Notaire tell you that you have a right of way to the river? Your predecessors could walk back and forth across the bottom of the garden to extract water from the river. That was the access point."

"We used to use it sometimes to go between the two gardens, saved having to go around via the road to borrow a rake or deliver a cake," Teen explained. Then in a whisper close to my ear, she added, "We could always use it at as secret pathway between the two of us if you want?!"

The idea appealed to the Enid Blyton fan in me, so I readily agreed. I must point out that I'm not so much Anne of the Famous Five, all goody-goody and making sure there are lashings of pop. No, I'm more like Janet in the Secret Seven. Like the members of the Secret Seven, I never went to boarding school, unlike my Aunty Gillian.

Aunty Gillian is my mother's younger sister, a bit of an afterthought in the family, she is only ten years older than me. Oh dear, this story is going to get complicated. I suppose I need to explain a little about my family history.

My mother was born in rural Wiltshire in 1934, second child of the family, three years younger than David, her brother. At the outbreak of war Grandfather, a Territorial (part-time, volunteer) Officer in the Royal West Wiltshire Rifles had been sent to Greece as of the Expeditionary Force in 1941. He was taken prisoner by the Italians and held until 1943 when they surrendered. He had left the prison camp before the German troops arrived to take over and headed south. Eventually, after weeks of living rough, he was taken in by a peasant family and sheltered with them, working in the fields until the allies drove north in 1944.

During the war years, Mother had stayed at home with Grandma and her brother, David. The large country house had been filled with young women. Some of the women had only stayed for a few days. Other women stayed for months, going out early in the morning, returning late in the evening. Very few of the women ever returned for a second stay.

I get the feeling it was some sort of spy school, but that is conjecture.

Grandfather was repatriated to Britain in 1945, and my mother soon had a new sister. My Aunty Gillian.

Tragedy struck the family eventually. I was never to meet my Uncle David. He was killed, leading the men of The Royal Wiltshire's in Korea.

My father had a very different war to my mother. His family were planters in Ceylon (now Sri Lanka) before and during the war. As a result of the war, he was educated locally up to the age of 14. With the end of hostilities, he was packed off to a boarding school in southern England. He hated it, the poor food, the cold, the loss of freedom and finally for the loss of his parents. They had moved to Malaya to help restart the country's rubber production and been caught 'up country' in the early days of the Malayan Emergency.

That might explain why I never went away to school. They both carried emotional scars caused by their own experiences and had worked hard to make sure that I, their only child, had a stable and happy childhood to compensate.

My Aunty Gillian was barely ten years older than me and as a result, she became my surrogate older sister while I was growing up. It was her Enid Blyton books that I used to spend weekends reading while she was away at school. It was Gillian who regaled me with stories of the dormitory and common room antics during her summer holidays. It was her books that I inherited when she discovered boys.

Gillian and I had remained close until she disappeared on a trek across Europe, I got a postcard from Greece. Then it appears she had travelled further East, being taken very ill in Kashmir. I heard about that in another postcard from Greece that arrived some eighteen months later. Even after she returned to the UK, started a family, got divorced and remarried, much of the tale of her adventures went untold.

I went to University, met Jerry and started my own family and we sort of lost touch. The years passed, we would exchange cards for birthdays and Christmas, with notes promising to meet or visit each other in the coming year.

We did meet at Nana's funeral, that was about fifteen years ago, Gillian had flown in from Spain where she and her husband live on 'some sort of farm', which they run as a Bed and Breakfast. It must be a very busy place; we had tried to book a visit several times, only to disappointed to discover that other guests were staying. On the other hand, she had promised to come and visit us in August, to escape the heat of Spain for a few days. With the proviso that we would have to put up with her bohemian, hippy ways.

When I'd mentioned that her Great Aunt would be coming to stay later in the summer, my darling daughter Denise had harrumphed and then snorted at the hippy ways bits. She had then refused to discuss it further saying Gillian was my Aunt and it was her story to tell. I deduced from that reaction that things had been discussed between the cousins (of sorts) and I remained outside the loop.

I woke from my daydream to realise the sunshine was finished for another day. The clouds were starting to thicken again as another belt of rain approached. We all trooped back into Ian and Teen's lounge, opened another bottle of red and chatted late into the night. Family Man

We chatted alright, drank a few bottles too.

I have only vague recollections of some of what we talked about. I have slightly less idea about how much we drank and no idea at all how come I have woken up in my bed, with my wife snoring next to me. I lay very still, counting my blessings for as long as possible, hoping the furriness of my tongue was not correlated with the severity of my impending headache.

It wasn't at all, I had the furriness, but as it transpired Fran had the headache! We spent a very quiet day doing very little, very quietly. Still, we had enjoyed getting to know all about the neighbours on one side of our new home. I am still a little concerned about what Roger said, I assume, about the people on the other side. Mind you, there has been no sight of them yet, maybe part two of the gossip he passed on is true.

The rest of the week we were busy getting ready for our son, Gavin, coming to stay for a long weekend with his girlfriend, Inga. They phoned on Monday evening and invited themselves for a long weekend, arriving Thursday and heading back late Monday. Gavin had met Inga while on one of these strange university courses that involve spending a year abroad. In his case, it was in the Business School in Maastricht. Inga was doing a similar business degree in the university in Uppsala, with a year in Maastricht. Their relationship survived their final years' at different universities, in different cities, in different countries. After they graduated, both had managed to land jobs in the City of London.

Not that I'm jealous of my son. I'm not, but I wish I had the same opportunities at his age, then it was never going to be easy for an almost orphan. An 'almost orphan'? I hear you ask. As it happens, it is the best description I can come up with for my situation. I'll explain.

The first three or four years of my life were, I suspect, outwardly normal. Then my father ran off with another woman. My mother, unable to cope on her own, had moved to London to find work, leaving me with my Grandparents. Then when I was eight, a letter arrived, informing Nana and Gramps that Mum had met a new man and they were emigrating to Australia, forever. She promised, that once they were established, she would send for me.

That letter never arrived.

Gramps and Nana did their best for me. I got into the local Technical High School. I never set the world of academia alight, but I managed to stay 'mid-table'. At sixteen I left school and got an apprenticeship with a local pharmaceutical firm. Then at eighteen, I started going to college in the evenings, took some more exams and suddenly they had me working in the production office.

It was around that time I met Fran, at the side of the road. Her car had broken down, it was chucking down with rain, she was driving a Mini, so I knew what the problem was. Damp in the electrics, there was nothing I could do there and then. Being a gentleman, and her being rather pretty, I towed her home and pushed the car into her father's garage. While the water repellent spray was doing its magic on the electrics, she brought me a cuppa. Then we went out to the pictures the following week. The rest is, as they say, history.

We already had Denise and Gavin when the firm I had worked for was taken over. The factory was going to be closed and production and all the machines moved to one of the 'Garden City' developments. For some reason, I got the job of planning the move. In the end, everything went very smoothly. The redundancy money was enough to keep us going for several months. Then one of the other chaps who had been laid off phoned. He had a new job with a firm that was expanding and was bringing in some new lines from another factory. He had put me forward as someone who could manage this type of move. After that, it was a job planning a move for the local hospital's Pharmacy Dept. Then, well I never escaped the hospital. Eventually, I got my own entry in the phone directory, J Tilson, Project Manager.

Wow, I was a Project Manager. Courses and qualifications followed. Promotions too, I was Head of Facilities and Services Development, a Project Manager with lots of projects.

I suppose it sounds good to you, from lowly beginnings and all that. What I find sad in it all is that in all that time I have never moved more than ten miles from the house I had grown up in. We had taken holiday trips all over Europe and even the USA, but I had never called anywhere else 'home'.

I know that is why it is so important to me to become part of this community, my first home away from home. Gavin had links now with three different countries.

Now Gavin and Inga must be on the verge of something new. They had asked to come to visit us at short notice because they have something they want to discuss with us. Fran was hoping it would involve her buying a new hat! Which just goes to show, that occasionally, even the highly developed feminine intuition my wonderful wife has can go astray.

I picked the youngsters up from the airport on Thursday evening. Fran was at home minding the (celebration) dinner she had spent two days planning and preparing. Even I could tell the two youngsters were tense. There was something major that they were going to announce.

Things remained tense and a little stiff, we had finished the starters (and a bottle of chilled rosé). At that point, I decided to take the tiger by the tail and grasping it firmly using it as a stick to beat the elephant in the room. If you don't mind me mixing a metaphor or three.

"So," I probed with great subtlety, "What is it you want to tell us?"

My finesse paid off and they started to talk. Gavin explained that things had been going well for both of them at work,. Fran looked disappointed to start with, but cheered up when it obviously wasn't going to be bad news. Inga had been doing so well that she had been offered a promotion. A promotion and a transfer to the Chicago office of her bank.

The downside was that the firm Gavin works for doesn't have an office anywhere in the Americas. Faced with a stark choice, do something or lose Inga, he had chosen to give up his job and start his own online business offering stock market tips and advice to investors. He was going to run it from the dining table of the apartment they were going to rent in the Windy City.

I could see the sense in this plan. They could stay together. Gavin could run his UK-based business from a laptop anywhere, so no need for a work permit. His CV would remain continuous, And, here's the big bit, it was what he was already, very successfully, doing, as a wage slave, for his current employers.

Fran was still very sad about the lack of opportunity to dash off to the milliners for something special.

"What was so urgent that you came to see us face to face to tell us about your new jobs?" She enquired.

"We, or rather I, was worried about how you would react to the news we were going to be moving thousands of miles away. I wanted you to understand that this isn't just a whim. I ..." Gavin ground to a halt.

"That's very kind of you son," I said slipping an arm around his shoulder, "It is your future. You must do what is best for both of you. That in part is why we are here, to allow you and your sister the room to stretch your wings and fly!"

This got me a great big hug from Inga, which I rather enjoyed and a big smile from Fran, which was even better. The rest of the evening was spent enjoying a celebratory dinner and talking excitedly about the new lives we all had in front of us.

Friday, we spent the day showing Gavin and Inga around the sites of interest in our new neighbourhood and introducing them to some of our new-found friends. Inga commented that we seemed to have settled into village life rather well, it reminded her of the way people in her hometown in Sweden interacted. When new arrivals came to live in the small town, everyone would gather and have a party to make introductions and welcome the newcomers, she explained to us as we drove home.

"A bit like a housewarming party," Gavin added, helping clarify Inga's explanation. Not that I thought it needed clarification, but it had triggered something inside Fran's head. I could tell, she went quiet for several minutes, while we pulled into our driveway.

The following day, we awoke to blazing sunshine. OK, I'll admit it, I woke up late, alone in bed, the sun streaming in through the open windows and the sounds of Fran's exercise regimen drifting up from the garden. A few moments later the sounds of the shower running alerted me to the fact that either Gavin or Inga was up and about too. Having missed my chance of a quick shower, I slipped on a pair of what the supermarket called 'leisure pants' and went to start the coffee machine. As I walked to the top of the stairs, I could make out Gavin's voice, singing in the shower. I assumed that Inga must still be in bed.

Wrong again, the joys of being a man. No sooner than I had sorted out the coffee maker and the first burst of that wonderful aroma had tickled my olfactory nerves, Inga appeared. Not as I might have expected from the direction of the bedroom, for which she was dressed, but from the garden.

"Fran says she will be here in a few minutes," She informed me, as she examined the progress of the coffee maker. The sight of that much leg! I understand why my son is willing to give up on his job and move halfway around the world. I suddenly realise I am almost jealous of my own son.

I was saved from further discomforting thoughts about my erstwhile daughter-in-law by the arrival of Fran. Who was draped in her loose silk kimono, flashing a lot of thigh as she walked across the kitchen. Legal naughty thoughts raced across my mind as I saw the smile on Fran's face.

We sat out on the terrace for breakfast, chatting about life in France and how different it was going to be from the city life the kids would be experiencing soon. Gavin then asked who else was going to be visiting us over the summer. Fran mentioned her Aunt Gillian was coming in August.

Gavin neatly choked on a mouthful of coffee. "Aunty Gillian, now that will be an experience for you!" He spluttered, "She leads a slightly different lifestyle to you two you know!"

"She did say that we would have 'have to put up with her bohemian, hippy ways.' I am prepared for an interesting few days," Fran responded.

"I'm sure you will have no problem accommodating her, Fran," Inga had a distinct smile showing in her eyes, "Although I'm not sure everyone would." I suspected that last comment was aimed at me.

"What makes you say that?" Fran enquired.

Gavin rolled his eyes slightly before replying, "We went to Gillian and Duncan's for a week last summer, with Cousin Will and his wife, Jackie. It was a just a little bit alternative. I think you must have been house hunting in France at the time," Gavin paused, "Let's just say that their place is not a run of the mill bed and breakfast, but I'll let her tell you all about it!"

Despite lots of prodding and questioning, Gavin declined to say any more. Inga just sat there smiling and refusing to say any more than Gavin. Eventually, Fran and I went for our showers. Gavin and Inga went over to the pool.

When I came down Fran was emerging from the pantry. She announced that we needed some bits and pieces from the shops for supper tomorrow. I had booked us into a nearby restaurant for Saturday night, but finding somewhere good to eat that opened on a Sunday evening was a bit of a nightmare. I grabbed the car keys while Fran went to tell 'les enfants' where we were going.

It was a couple of hours later when we got back from shopping. I helped carry the bags in from the car. Then while Fran was putting the groceries away, I went to see if Gavin and Inga wanted a drink.

As I approached the pool, Gavin must have spotted me while he was swimming and called out to me. As I returned the greeting, I saw Inga rolling over on a sunbed, I guessed she was topless. To avoid staring, I talked directly to Gav, who was now against the side of the pool. Having taken the drinks order, I went back to the house to pour them.

"I think I nearly caught Inga sunbathing topless," I observed to Fran as I opened the beers.

"Really dear, that doesn't surprise me."

We carried the drinks and some snacks out to the terrace between us. Gavin and Inga joined us, walking from the pool with towels wrapped around them like sarongs. I noticed that Inga had no shoulder straps and whispered to Fran, "See!"

Fran rolled her eyes and scooped up a handful of nuts.

Mother, daughter-in-law moment

Rolled my eyes, you bet I did! I don't know what it is with my husband and topless sunbathers. We have been coming to the Continent for our holidays for more than twenty years. Every year he goes ga-ga over the first topless woman, other than me, he sees. Then twenty-four hours later it is as if he was bored with the sight of bare-breasted women. One of them is a subconscious acting out, I'm just not sure which one.

One thing I am fairly sure of, following this morning, is that Inga was probably at least topless. I haven't told Jerry about my exercise session earlier, yet! I see no reason to either, he is being so juvenile at the moment.

I was up early, doing my usual stretching regimen out in the garden, when Inga had wandered up and started chatting about the exercises I was doing, why I had chosen each exercise, why was I doing exercises, naked, in the garden at this time of day? The fact that she was sat on the grass in just a short dressing gown enabled me to overcome my embarrassment and continue to run through my programme, while answering her. I suppose it is to do with her being Swedish that makes it all acceptable. From that point, I should expect Gavin will have adjusted to make allowances for her lifestyle choices. I wonder just how much by way of allowances? And just how 'bo-ho' my hippy Aunt really is? It can't be that radical surely, after all her son, Will, seemed normal enough when he stayed with us for a week last year.

The rest of the afternoon was spent sitting in the sun, beer in hand, telling tales of Gavin's youth. All for Inga's benefit, naturally. The truth was, of course, we rather enjoyed reliving our younger days. Mind you Inga did rather egg us on!

I must give Jerry due credit; the restaurant was excellent. We had a wonderful meal served in a perfect setting with a great atmosphere. We staggered indoors and all went straight to bed.

In the morning it was already hot by the time I woke up, Jerry was still asleep, as usual. I slipped out of bed and into my kimono, don't ask me why I wear my kimono normally, but today it is because I might have bumped into Gavin on the landing, I didn't. In the kitchen, I got myself a glass of water then wandered off to my outdoor gym.

"Hello!" I nearly dropped the glass in surprise. Then I see Inga sitting in the lotus position, naked, under the shade of one of the trees. "Do you mind if I join you this morning? This is a wonderful place for meditation but now I feel the need for movement."

Well, what can you say when you are confronted by your not-quite-daughter-in-law dressed ready to join you in your naked exercise regimen? I mean apart from, "Of course you can."

I turned on the ambient soundtrack from my phone and we worked our way smoothly through a sequence of Sun Salutations into Downward Facing Dogs, walking out into the Plank, holding it for a few minutes before lowering and up into the Cobra. Then after relaxing in the Baby Pose for a few minutes rebuilding by reversing the routine. Repeating the cycle a few times then chilling, watching the trees move against the clear, blue sky until we were ready to start the day.

It was Sunday, it was hot, so we went to the beach. Jerry and I were both rather surprised when Gavin suggested that we should head for Sérignan beach. I didn't think he knew the area at all, but he had some app on his phone, so Sérignan it was.

When we got there, it turned out to be a big sandy beach, backed by campsites. We got set up and comfortable. Jerry had his Kindle and I had a pile of magazines that Inga had thoughtfully collected up for me. We settled down to read when the youngsters announced that they were going for a walk along the beach. With that they picked up their towels and walked off to the south, well Jerry told me it was south.

"It's a bit early for Lovebirds to be migrating south for the winter," were his actual words.

It was hours later before they came back. They appeared to have had a good time, they were laughing and joking and had been swimming, judging by Inga's wet, tousled hair. We shared a couple of pastries we had bought on the journey to the beach and a couple of bottles of the rapidly warming beer.

After lunch Jerry suggested a swim, Inga demurred, saying she didn't want to get her bikini wet. It occurred to me that was strange as she had been swimming earlier, but before I could focus on the thought, it was washed from my mind. Jerry had grabbed me from behind and thrown me into an oncoming wave. It wasn't a big wave, but I hit it in such a way that my top was displaced. Bosoms akimbo, I spluttered to my feet, unhitched my top and started to hit him with the soggy cups, amid much laughter.

I must point out, I seldom wear a bikini top on the beach, but I was today, out of some sort of concern about the presence of my son. I had the feeling Inga was only wearing her top, by the same sort of logic, because of Jerry.

Hours later, as we sat on the terrace watching the sun setting, replete from eating coq-au-vin, that had been slow cooking for over twelve hours, we all agreed it had been a great day. Jerry raised a glass to toast Gavin's inspired choice of beach and we all drank to that. Then, the cicadas' song ceased, and the sun slipped into fiery oblivion below the hills to the west. It was almost the end of Gavin and Inga's first and potentially last, at least for a while, visit to our new home in France.

Jerry and I left them with the last half bottle of the rosé and went to bed. A little later, I thought I heard laughter and splashing from the pool. I fell asleep, thinking about trying to dry damp bikinis.

In the morning I got up to do my stretches and found Inga waiting in the same position as the day before. We ran through the same routine, then sat in the warm morning sun and had a girlie talk. What were her plans for the future? Would I have any grandchildren? Should I buy that hat just in case?

In return I got: they have all been turned upside down; more than likely; and not yet. All delivered with an impish smile that suggested I had missed something. I got deflected from pressing for more answers when Inga asked me about my relationship with Gillian. It was a harmless question, so I told her about my surrogate elder sister. Her going off on her travels and never quite managing to get back as close as we had been. Inga listened to my tale then announced we should go for breakfast.

Later, while we were waiting for their flight back to London to be called, I asked Inga why she was so interested in the relationship between Gillian and me. "Oh, it was just something Gillian had said while we were staying in Spain, and the fact Gillian was suddenly coming to see you in August. It made me wonder." The enigmatic smile played across Inga's lips; their flight was called through and I never got to ask the follow-up question.

Another toy!

I must be getting better at this pool maintenance lark! I got up this morning expecting to have to deal with a cloudy pool, but no, it is still as clear as crystal. Just as well, it was going to be a really hot one today. We were going to need the pool to keep our cool. I should be a poet for that, 'We need a pool to keep our cool.' Brilliant, but where to next? The only other rhyming word I could think of was 'fool', that would make me sound like Mr T, from the A-Team series.

I was setting up the sun loungers and the parasol when I heard splashing from next door. We weren't the only ones 'Keepin' ah cool in da pool!' Maybe I could become a rapper? No, the baggy trousers wouldn't look good on me!

A little later, while Fran and I were sitting quietly reading, there was a "Coo-ee!" from the bottom of the garden and Teen appeared through the gate. Moments later as we exchanged *bisous,* I became aware that not only was Fran topless in front of our neighbour and totally at ease, but our neighbour probably was too under the light sundress she was wearing.

"We need a favour," I love conversations that begin like that! "We are off up to Paris for a few days, to pick up our American friends. Will you keep an eye on the pool, Jerry?"

There I am being trusted with a pool! Ian must have noticed that I hadn't needed to shock our pool after this weekend.

"Of course, anything else we can do?"

"If you don't mind Fran, can you pop over at some time to water the plants, please? This heat is drying them up so fast!"

"No problem, can you get them all collected into one area, so I don't miss any though?"

A few minutes later and we had agreed the details, we were in charge, as of the following evening. Fran walked Teen back towards the gate discussing whatever women discuss at times like this.

As the afternoon passed, the temperature continued to rise. It seemed to get hotter still after the sunset. By bedtime, it was impossible to go to sleep. After we had been trying to get to sleep for half an hour, Fran leapt off the bed.

"I'm off for a swim, it's bound to be cooler than lying here!" And off she went! With me trying to find something to wear, trailing behind her. I couldn't find anything, Fran was not wearing anything, so, 'when in Rome' I thought, besides, it was dark and you can't see the pool from the neighbours' houses.

It was the first time I had ever skinny dipped. And wow, it felt so liberating. I knew there was a reason we had insisted on a pool! I think that Fran enjoyed the experience too, judging by the amount of time she spent just floating with an inflatable pillow supporting her head. I spent much of the time sitting on the edge of the pool, feet trailing in the water, looking at the stars. It was rather peaceful, except when I got rather excited as the International Space Station crossed the sky, looking like a silver cross. I had to apologise to Fran for letting the Inner Nerd escape, but she agreed it was a splendid sight. We must have been out there for a couple of hours, just lounging around in the cool water.

Eventually, the yawns started to

become too frequent to hide them and it was time for bed again. This time sleep came quickly and with it the dawn.

While I showered, Fran went off to do her stretches. By the time she was showered and fragrant, I was back from the boulangerie with some fresh pastries. As we munched on the pain-au-chocs, in the sunshine of another warm morning, I remembered.

"I saw Ian and Teen down the road, as they were leaving. They have just had delivery of some clever device for cleaning the bottom of the pool. They said we could try it. The box is by the flowers. I thought I'd pick it up later this morning and we could water the plants then too?"

"Sounds like a plan!" Fran agreed, "But it will have to be sooner rather than later, or it will be too hot for watering."

We popped the mugs and plates into the dishwasher and set off through the gate. The box was exactly where they said it would be. It only took a few minutes to water the plants, there weren't that many. I suppose it must be almost impossible to keep plants growing when you are away as much as the neighbours seem to be. I decided that I would try out the gadget immediately.

"Boys and their toys!" I heard Fran mutter. "Try not to break it. I'll go home and get the bedsheets washed. They'll dry in no time!"

I could feel a gentle breeze that had been absent the day before, as I carried the book down to Ian's pool. I unpacked the device. It looked like some sort of rotary brush, powered by water from a hose connected to the pool pump. I laid the pieces out on the pool surround and instead of doing my usual put it together first, then read the instructions to find out why it wasn't working, I was going to read the instructions first!

The instructions, where were the instructions? I'd put them down just ... Oh! There they are. In the pool, slowly sinking. They were out of reach. The pool tools were in the shed and it was locked.

'I'm going to have to go in and get them, but I've got my best shorts on. I mustn't get them soaked. I'll have to take them off.' My brain was racing; within moments I was stripped to my underpants. 'Urgh, soggy underwear! What the hell, there is no one to see.' I amazed myself when I realised that there

I was, less than twelve hours after my first skinny dip, swimming *au natural* in our neighbours' pool. They were away and unlikely to catch me, but it did add a frisson of excitement to the event.

Fortunately, the instructions were a single sheet and they would dry out quickly as I followed them. Aided by the diagrams, I soon had all the bits hooked together and I was just about to lower it into the pool when Fran returned.

"I was just coming to remind you to change out..." She had caught sight of my naked nether regions. "What a good idea! Cleaning the pool in the buff, I was going to suggest that you change out of your new shorts before you ruin them. You have several pairs with bleach marks on them already!"

"I'd noticed that too," I lied, "So I thought I'd dispense with clothes for the pool cleaning while we are alone." Then it hit me, it had seemed like a good move, but now I was going to have to follow through on the idea.

Of course, I couldn't try out the gadget, all the pipes, handles and the pool controls were locked in the shed. I was going to have to take it to our place for a trial, I explained, as Fran was gathering up my clothes.

"No problem, slip your shoes back on, I'll carry your clothes, and you can bring the device."

Fran was suggesting that I walked around to our house bare, carrying the pool cleaner. Before a message could get from my brain to my mouth, Fran was on her way with my clothes. I had no alternative but to trail along behind in flip-flops.

It wasn't that bad I suppose, nobody was watching and, well, nothing fell off. I got the cleaner to our pool, then went and fetched the hoses and poles from our shed. Hooked it all up, lowered it into the pool. Everything in place I went to switch on the pump.

I came back in time to see the end of the pole disappearing into the water as the device started to move. Fortunately, I was suitably dressed for getting into the pool and was able to take control very quickly. I ran the cleaner around our pool, by the finish, I know I have saved us a few euros. The wonder gadget wasn't any better than my old brush. Thank goodness, I have had the chance to try this thing out at someone else's expense.

I went and got dressed again, but into an older pair of trousers! Better for tidying up the garden, I was still clearing clippings from the trees out of the 'lawn' to make it safer for feet. There were so many jobs to be done and now it was too hot to do many of them between early morning and early afternoon.

By eleven, I'd stopped and was sitting in the shade of a tree, sipping a cup of tea. It was black tea, I still can't cope with UHT milk in tea, but it was more refreshing than coffee. Fran was just getting the dry washing in off the line, her wrap shifting slightly in the breeze from the outside and the movement of her body from within. I could have spent ages watching her, but I was spotted and called to help fold the sheets.

By the time the evening arrived the breeze was stronger and the temperature was more comfortable. We were both tired from the recent late nights. Sleep came easily.

Plans made, plans changed

The breeze was still there when I woke up, refreshed after a good night's sleep. We both had jobs to get done, I had some shutter painting to finish. Jerry still had a big patch of weeds to whack. We needed an early start. I gave Jerry a shove. Much to my surprise, Jerry was already awake.

"I was thinking," He said.

"Dangerous!"

"I was thinking," He continued, so I listened this time, "If we get up and get straight on, we can clean up and shower afterwards, instead of getting all sweaty after we shower."

It made sense, up to a point. "When am I going to do my exercises? And when will the pool cleaning get done?" Jerry had an answer for that too. He had been thinking.

"It's about seven now, if we get up, grab a coffee and get on, we can get a couple of hours in by half-nine. If we stop then, you can do your exercises while I sort out breakfast, then after breakfast, you shower while I do the pool. Then I can shower. All done ready for the day by eleven," He concluded.

"That sounds like a plan!" I leapt out of bed. "I'll go and get the coffee on while you get into your protective gear." I was laughing at the thought of that pair of socks as I dashed to the bathroom.

We worked like Trojans for those few hours. Then almost to the minute, we stopped and had breakfast. Jerry is good at this planning thing!

When I arrived poolside, with my wet hair wrapped loosely in a towel turban, Jerry was just putting everything away. I was slightly surprised to see him stripped to do the cleaning, as he had promised. Mind you, when I gathered up his work clothes I kind of understood, I would want out of them.

I sorted out my hair, while Jerry showered. Then we settled down to a quiet day. The sun continued to shine, it was very warm, and the day was very peaceful. I found myself dozing. Jerry woke with a start when he dropped his Kindle.

"How about we go and have a siesta?" I suggested. I didn't need to ask twice. I have no idea what Jerry was expecting.

It was still very hot when we decided it was time to get moving again. We chose to have a late lunch, or early dinner. I made us a large salad, which we ate, sitting on chairs by the pool. We washed it down with a bottle of white wine. All very nice, I'd never eaten a meal wearing so little. When the dressing dipped down my front, I just laughed, rather than having to mop furiously at the mark.

It was getting too dark to read when we decided it was time to give up on the pool. The insects were starting to buzz around, despite the repellent, so we went indoors and to bed. It had been a very long day.

The siesta had messed up my sleep rhythm. I started thinking about what Inga had said about having a housewarming party. It seemed like a very sensible idea, but when? My shuffling around must have woken Jerry.

"What's keeping you awake?"

"Brain race, stuff going in my mind." Strangely we were both whispering.

"Mainly about a housewarming party for the villagers and some of the expats."

"Fine," Jerry whispered, "When are you thinking of having this do?"

"That is what's keeping me awake, when can we fit it in?"

Jerry suggested sooner, so it was all over and done with, before Gillian was due. I had thought later so we had more time to prepare things. Jerry explained his logic and it made sense.

I'm one of those people who worries about entertaining, I try to micro plan for every eventuality. As a result, I get stressed. Jerry pointed out that I was already stressing about Gillian's visit, some four weeks away.

"If we have the party after her visit, you will be stressing about the party for at least five weeks. Which will include all of the precious time that your Aunt is with us." He was right about that. "If we arrange the party before she comes, not only is there less time for worrying about it, but it will be all over and you can have time to focus on getting ready for your Aunt's visit exclusively!"

Well, since he put it like that, I had to agree, I suppose. Jerry declared the best day to be the third Sunday from today. Then he rolled over and went straight back to sleep. Problem solved, as far as he was concerned. I was working on the buffet menu and who to invite deep into the night.

After my morning stretches (I can now bend over and get the palms of my hands flat on the ground), I retired to a sun lounger to formulate some plans. I had lists sorted out and written by lunchtime.

I wandered into the kitchen to see what we were going to have with our bread and cheese. I could hear Jerry was either on Skype or the phone, talking very loudly. He sounded frustrated rather than angry, thank goodness. Suddenly his tone changed and the volume dropped.

I went and fished the cheese out of the fridge and put it onto the board. Yes, we know the fridge kills the flavour but ... and I do get it out first, so it has a chance to warm up. I sorted out a mixed salad. Yes, tomatoes in the fridge too. I finished by adding a few olives and chopped jalapeños to give it a little fizz. I could hear Jerry winding up his call as I cut the bread.

I had just carried everything out to the table, when Jerry emerged from the house. I knew something was up when he pulled me towards his chest and gave me a kiss.

"Looking fabulous, darling," He said. I'm not sure if he meant the food, or my breasts, from the direction of his eyes! Just in case it was me, I gave a little shimmy. It might well have been me, Jerry's smile got a little broader as we sat down.

It didn't take long for him to come to the point. He was buttering his first chunk of crispy bread when he announced.

"I am going back to England for a couple of days."

"Oh?" That was rather unexpected, we were supposed to have retired to do things together.

"It has all gone tits-up at work, they need me to go in and sort it out. I need to go in tomorrow and the next day to analyse the problem. Then it will be a couple of weeks, working from here, to plan the changes. After that, I will have to go back to the UK to do some training, another five days in September." He paused, while I assimilated this news. "Lots of good news then isn't it?"

More plans

I was surprised that Fran failed to recognise how clever I had been immediately. I'll never understand why women can't see how cunning and devious us men can be.

"We have nothing on, well you have very little on!" I teased Fran gently about the fact she appeared to only have her bikini bottoms and a wrap around her hips. "No, seriously, we have nothing planned, or on the must do list. I'm away one night, that's all.

"I'll be in a hotel and you will have lots of time to get on with party planning." She nodded, showing that made sense to her. "I can do the report and planning at my own pace, at times to suit us. Like when it is too hot to sit out!"

"Then there is the week in September," She interjected.

"Ah, yes, the all-expenses-paid week in a double room in a four-star hotel a few miles up the road from Denise and the boys, what about it?"

"When in September would this be?"

She was cottoning on to how clever I had been. Then I revealed that I arranged it for late in the month. After all, it had to be after everybody had returned from their holidays and the children were settled in their new schools. Suddenly, Fran realised just how clever I had been. Henry's birthday is the 24th September and James's on the 28th. Fran and I had jokingly worked out what Denise's ex-husband liked to have as a Christmas present!

I had deliberately omitted to tell Fran just how very obscene my daily rate was going to be. It was going to be the trump card, but I didn't need to play it to win this trick. I'll use it to win another hand later in the game of life. For example, Fran has always wanted to go to the Caribbean, guess what she is getting for her Christmas present! No, not that! I might if have played this card right though!

Slightly earlier than the crack of doom next morning, we set off to Toulouse, where I caught the early flight to Gatwick. Almost before Fran got back home, I was on the train to the office. My goodness, it was cold out though, about ten degrees colder.

By the close of business the next day,

I had a pretty good idea about what had gone wrong. They hadn't listened to me the first time around! It had gone, as I predicted it would go, badly. Writing the recovery plan would just be a case of re-dating my original proposals. Well, there was a little more than that to it, but nothing drastic needed changing! I got back to Toulouse a little before midnight to discover that Fran had been shopping. Somehow she had found out the famous Swedish furniture shop has a branch in Toulouse. Still, there was enough space for me and my overnight bag in amongst the new garden table and chairs. I knew what my main job for tomorrow was going to be.

As we drove up the road to the house, we noticed the car was back on the drive at Ian and Teen's place. At least I didn't have to go watering and pool cleaning for them as well as everything else in the morning.

A big surprise

We woke up late, well Jerry did. I had already done my stretches for the morning before I took the cups of coffee up to bed. Not that it mattered at all, I was getting the hang of this laid-back lifestyle.

Once we finally got started, Jerry was amazing. Started assembling the furniture! I'm beginning to think Jerry is right about you lot having dirty minds. He was putting the flat-pack furniture together and moving it around the garden until I was happy with it. The truly amazing thing was, that he did it all without complaining once.

Once everything was in its place, we relaxed by the pool for the rest of the afternoon. I felt that Jerry had earnt a little break, as it was, he spent the time reading something on his laptop. Every so often, he would chuckle, type for a few moments, then rub his hands together. That was all I needed to know. The hand rubbing behaviour is a tell for Jerry being pleased with himself. He had been shown to be right about something. I could only guess it was to do with the trip back to the UK.

I left him to it until supper, after that I needed his undivided attention for about half an hour, or longer, if I could get him engaged. In the garden it was still nice and warm when I laid the table for our evening meal. I called to Jerry to come to the new table, while I went in to collect the wine and the insect repellent for Jerry. I'd given myself a spray when I had changed out of my swimming gear into one of Jerry's older white work shirts, they are nice and lose and just long enough to preserve an air of mystery.

I sprayed the old man's arms, chest back and legs until all the hairs were coated in the anti-mosquito mix. However, even before I had finished cutting the bread, he was all of a fidget on his chair. I offered him the serving spoons for the salad and he was on his feet, spooning leaves, tomatoes, cucumber, peppers and onion slices on to his plate. When he sat back down, it was only a few mouthfuls later that the squirming started again.

"For goodness sake Jerry! What is it have you got ants in your pants or something? Have you been bitten already?" I couldn't cope with him twitching like that and I needed him to concentrate later.

"No, I think it is the mesh lining of these swimming shorts. It is cutting into me something rotten!"

"Well, take them off silly! There is nobody watching and you can wrap the towel around you if you are that worried about me seeing you." A memory flashed through my mind.

Back in the early days of digital photography, we, like everybody else, I guess, took some pictures for our personal collection. Then, when we got the first smart TV, we copied all our holiday pictures onto a memory stick to use as a screen saver, remember screensavers? I'll never forget them. Jerry had removed all his personal collection of pictures of me after a few shots of me topless on assorted beaches graced a dinner party. He, however, forgot to remove the 'Fran's Faves' folder.

My mother had come to visit and we had the radio on. Via the TV. I went to make tea for the two of us. I think Jerry was doing something with one of the children. He often did that while my mother was visiting.

As I was saying, the radio was playing. I had been making tea and when

I came back, my mother was sitting forward on the settee, remote control in hand, pressing a button every few seconds. I looked at the TV and nearly dropped the tray. There on the screen was one of my favourite pictures of Jerry. He was walking towards the camera with a wicked smile on his face, stark naked with one of his very best erections leading the way.

"Now I understand what you see in that man!" My mother had a twinkle in her eye as she pushed the slideshow back again. "Your Dad would have been proud of one like that!"

"Mum, more information than I need!"

"Tush, girl! I saw a lot more than that when I was younger and closer up too! You, youngsters, didn't invent sex you know!" She sighed. "We were lucky in that we had Polaroid cameras, mind you, they were very expensive to use. The pictures faded over time, just like memories, too. In your Grandma's day, it was a case of Grandad borrowing a friend's darkroom for an evening. I hate to think how they paid for it! But yes," she brightened, "We had fun!"

I still have the one very blurred three-inch black and white picture of my mother lying naked on her sofa tucked in one of the old albums. I found it in her bedside draw while we were emptying her house. It was in an envelope with three or four other pictures, one of which might have been my Dad.

"Earth to planet Fran, come in planet Fran!"

"Sorry, I was just remembering a conversation with my mother. How's your bum feeling now?"

"Much better, my 'bottom' feels less 'puck'-ered." He smiled, he was very considerate about how sensitive I remained about Mum's rather sudden death. "A fresh glass of wine?"

Later, we sat back in our new garden chairs, dirty plates and glasses of wine on the table and went through my list of people to invite to our soiree, or was it going to be an apero, or just a party. It took surprisingly little time to agree that the weekend after next, we would be hosting a housewarming 'Aperaty'. All the Expat crowd, the tug of war team, the Cheerleader Crew and the crowd from the bar were going to be invited. It sounds a lot of people, but the Cheerleaders were married to the tug-of-war team. The tug-of-war team are regulars at the bar, where many of the expats could be found drinking. In all, we were inviting about forty new friends to help celebrate our arrival in our new home.

The second part of my agenda was almost as easy, the evening sun and chilled wine had mellowed Jerry. Drinks, we agreed to limit it to a choice from: beer, three colours of the local wine, a selection of soft drinks or fruit juice plus a choice of still and sparkling water. The food caused a bit more discussion, before we decided to do a 'Tapas' type thing. Strangely it was very similar to the leaving party we had hosted in our nearly empty house before we left England.

Jerry went to fetch a second bottle of rosé from the fridge, leaving his towel behind. I was a little disappointed when he returned, he was looking very relaxed. A little later I had changed that, as we snuggled together on the garden swing.

The following morning, I got on the computer and designed an invitation that we printed off and addressed by hand. We scanned the invitation for a few of the more distant expats and e-mailed their invitations. Then I took my life in my hands and sent Jerry off to the bar to distribute most of the remainder.

One of the few cards left was for Teen and Ian, they were only next door, I could drop it round now. Seeing as I was dressed for the pool rather than the road I decided to take the Secret Seven's secret passage. I slipped another of Jerry's white shirts over my bikini and headed through our gate into the vineyard beyond. So far, so good. I was glad I had my flipflops on my feet as the ground looked very rocky and was covered with weeds. I made my way cautiously over to the gate at the bottom of Teen's garden and pushed it open. No problem! I walked into the garden and onto the path towards the house. Then, well then, I got the surprise of my life! Over by the pool, a man stood up. A tall, black man. By tall, I mean the sort of man who stands in front of me at concerts, all six-foot-six of him. And all six and a half feet of him was naked. I couldn't help but think that my mother would have lost all respect for Jerry if she were here.

"Hi!" he called out in a surprisingly melodic voice, "Are you looking for Teen and Ian?"

I nodded, unsure of quite where to

look then another, a female voice came from the same direction.

"Teen just went up to the house, she went to get some water for us." A comparatively petite, but comfortably upholstered, lady of colour was speaking to me from a sunbed near the pool in a cultivated American accent.

"Oh, thanks. I just wanted to … "I waved the invitation in the air as if it was an 'All Areas' pass. Just then Teen appeared from the kitchen to rescue me, I hoped.

"John, can you take the tray, please?" The big man moved past me and took the tray from her. "Is that for us?" She gestured towards to my talismanic piece of card, clutched in my hand, "Come up to the house and tell me about it!" She led me up the garden path; was this a metaphor, I wondered? Still clutching my 'Get Out of Jail (almost) Free' card in my hand. I wasn't quite sure where that almost went, 'Almost Get Out' 'Get Almost …' I trailed along behind Teen.

I had recovered some of my composure back by the time we reached the kitchen table. Teen was making coffee, as I started to burble.

"Sorry, I forgot you had guests, I was a bit startled ... "

"By a naked, two-metre-tall man suddenly appearing in front of you?"

"Well yes, he is very big and imposing!"

Teen burst out laughing. "Imposing, that is a good word for John! He is the guy Ian does business with, we told you about him."

"I remember, but you omitted any physical description. I'm sure I'd have remembered if you had told me Ian's business contact was a built like a 'jock', I believe the word is?" Adding to myself, "A naked jock at that."

"Well, he isn't always naked, nor is Lauren! If you remember Ian talking about soap and other stuff from costumes being what messes up a pool, we avoid it by simply swimming without one.
Afterwards, when it is hot and sunny, it makes sense to sit on towel-draped sunbeds to dry off." She broke off as the kettle boiled to make a couple of cups of instant coffee.

"Come down and say hello to John

and Lauren. Here, take your cup."

"I'll leave your invitation on the table!" I called as my hostess swept out of the kitchen. I dropped the card on the table and dashed after Teen as she walked towards the pool. As I hurried along, it occurred to me that my neighbour wasn't wearing much more than me.

At the pool, John was in the water floating on his back looking very relaxed. He waved as Teen did the introductions. I waved back with what I hoped was a smile. Lauren was sitting on the edge of her sunbed with a multi-coloured sarong wrapped around her.

"Hi Honey," She said in her well-modulated voice, "I just love that baggy shirt look. I wish I could find a man who wears a shirt big enough for me!" She laughed, her frame oscillating under her sarong causing it to come undone. "It would stop that from happening for a start!" She laughed again.

Teen gestured to me to sit on one of the sunbeds. We sat and chatted about the weather and transatlantic flights and French wines, all non-controversial subjects. At some stage, John had climbed out of the pool and laid down on a lounger, opened his Kindle and started to read.

I was talking to Lauren about my son and almost daughter-in-law moving to Chicago. She was telling me about their living in the city some ten years earlier, when I heard a splash. Teen had slipped into the water.

"Good idea, it's getting hot out here. Coming?" Lauren was on her feet undoing her wrap. I looked at John who appeared to have dozed off. Ah well, when in Rome, I suppose. I slipped off my bikini bottoms and pulled the shirt over my head. I scuttled to the poolside and slipped into the safety of the water. It was just like the other day in our pool, free and liberating.

I stayed in the water for a quarter of an hour or so, before getting out. A few minutes in the sun and I was able to pull the shirt back on. I said 'bye to Lauren and see you later to Teen. I was starting out of the pool gate when John called out, "Nice to have met you, Ma'am!"

He was awake! Never mind, no harm done. "Nice to meet you too, John, I hope to see you again someday." Why did I mention 'seeing' him again? I hurried home, got myself a glass of beer and went to the pool to wait for Jerry to return.

I was getting myself comfortable, mattress straight, towels in place, glass on the table and reached to slip the shirt back off … no bikini! I'd left it by the pool next door. 'Oh, sod it, there is no one else here!' and got comfortable.

When Jerry staggered back from the bar and several house visits, he woke me up. I had fallen asleep in the sun. I pulled the shirt on and went to get Jerry a coffee, the big, strong, black, coffee he needed. By the time I got back, with a pair of bikini bottoms on under the shirt, he was snoring.

That was rather convenient, because at that moment Teen appeared from the bottom of the garden. With my errant swimwear held in her fingers.

"You forgot something!" She announced as she approached.

I put my finger to my lips and pointed to the slumbering Jerry. I put the cup of coffee down on the ground beside him, straightened up and beckoned Teen to follow me. I led the way back towards the house. Away from Jerry and the risk of us waking him and ending up in a conversation about why I had abandoned my swimwear beside the neighbours' pool!

Cometh the drink

It had been a rather eventful trip around the village. Just as well I had walked. Everyone was delighted to be invited and offered me a drink by way of thanks. I was truly relieved to find a cool cup of coffee by the chair I had collapsed into when I got back.

I drank it in a single, continuous draft. I felt better as the caffeine started to circulate. I looked around for Fran. I caught sight of her laughing with Teen up by the house. I hoped I wasn't the butt of the joke. Deciding that maintaining a low profile would be the best strategy, I closed my eyes and dozed off again.

I heard Fran coming down the path with Teen. As they drew level, I made an effort, calling out a cheery, "I hope to see you soon!?"

After Fran came back, I managed to get on to my feet and followed her to the kitchen for a long drink of water and another coffee. Fran was remarkably gentle with me. I think she must have understood how difficult it would have been to escape from all of our friends without having a few drinks...

She sent me off to have a shower while dinner was being put together. I must admit that I felt a good deal more human after the shower. I dried off, put on my dressing gown and went back to the kitchen. Fran had some pasta on the boil, ready for making her famous pasta salad. The other ingredients were scattered across the table ready for prepping. I asked if she wanted any help. I was instructed to take a jug of fruit juice and a bottle of water out to the table and to wait.

I had nearly finished both by the time the food arrived on the table. I was now feeling a lot better and my head was starting to clear. I managed supper fairly well, I think. Then I fell asleep again.

When I woke up it was around sunset, Fran was shaking my shoulder and I was itching in several places. I'd not applied the insect repellent after my shower. Ah well, we still have plenty of anti-histamine cream in the cabinet.

With plenty of bite cream applied, I went to bed, where Fran soon joined me. She was in a rather frisky mood; thanks to my earlier nap I was able to respond appropriately! I also forgot all about the mossie bites…result!

The Start of the War

I slept soundly, Jerry had dealt with my itching very effectively. The sun was filtering through the gaps in the shutters. I ran through my checklist as I lay there. The invites were out, the menu and the drinks planned. No visitors coming to stay until Aunty Gillian. Shopping for the food, I would do that next Wednesday. The drinks, buying them the Saturday before the 'Aperaty' would be best, avoiding the temptation to get into quality control testing.

After my exercises, I was getting some yoghurt and fruit out for breakfast when I heard Jerry in the bathroom. I flicked the switch to start the coffee machine, plunged the toaster and went to the pantry for the jam and peanut butter.

You know, Jerry was right about the pantry. It is a wonderful thing. I walk in and there spread out in front of me are all the tins and jars that are normally hidden at the back of high shelves in kitchen cabinets. Now, instead of rummaging around hoping to find ingredients, I walk into the pantry and the ingredients compete with each other to be used!

We talked as we munched nutty-butty on toast. I wanted to make sure that the invitations had all been distributed. For all I knew, Jerry might have got stuck at the bar and still have a lot of the cards in his pocket. I asked how things had gone in a round-about way, always best with men I find.

"How many of the people we have invited weren't in yesterday?"

"I managed to deliver more than half of the invites into peoples' hands. If they were all being honest, we are going to have a great turn out. Hence the number of drinks I was offered! The rest, I delivered to peoples' homes. Can you pass the butter please?"

That would suggest that it was a case of mission accomplished. I passed the butter and another slice of toasted bread.

Jerry paused to have a slurp of coffee and asked how I had got on.

"I took the invitation around to Teen and Ian," I replied. "Oh yes, I met their American friends, John and Lauren. My goodness, John is a big man. He is well over six-foot tall and as they put it in the movies, over 250 pounds. Lauren is a bundle of fun too."

Jerry must have been in better shape than I thought, he remembered seeing Teen in our garden. Tricky, but fortunately, Jerry gave me some inspiration as he started to scratch an insect bite on his calf.

"She came around with a few web addresses for places selling mosquito nets and screens," I lied outrageously. "We had been talking about the difficulty of getting to sleep in the hot weather. Especially when you can't have the windows open."

"Good idea, were you thinking of an over the bed one, like they have in the old movies?" Jerry had taken the false trail. Fortunately, I had seen some window screens at Brico-Jardin and done a little research before Gavin and Inga's visit had pushed it to the back of my mind.

"They do look so romantic don't they?" I decided to follow this tangent, moving away from yesterday afternoon, "The problem is getting in and out of bed, in the middle of the night, without getting trapped like a fish in a net."

"Plus, you have all the little bastards

waiting to get you just outside the bed!" Jerry was still scratching, at something on his shoulder now.

"That's why I was thinking of having some window screens for the bedrooms, the landing and the bathroom." I worried this was sounding too much like a real plan. On the other hand…
"I think that would be a really good idea, do you want me to do some costings?" Jerry liked the idea and was ready to run with it. "I'll get on the net and find out how much they would be!"

It can't have been too expensive, a few hours later Jerry called out, "I'm off to the brico, I'll be back for lunch!"

I slipped out to call next door. I went around to the front so as not to get stuck talking to John and Lauren. It was important to make sure that Teen was singing from the same song sheet as me about her visit yesterday.

"You don't have fly screens on the windows?" Teen was amazed at the story I cooked up. "You'll notice just how much difference it makes to your sleep from night one!"

Well, that was a turn up for the books!

Jerry was back as promised in time for lunch. Tucked under his arm were three long boxes, well two long boxes and one very long box.

"I thought we could experiment with the three windows, our bedroom, the landing and the bathroom." I must have looked a bit blank at his logic. He continued, "That way we can secure the night-time trip to the bathroom. Provided, of course, we shut the other doors onto the landing."

Clever, sometimes it is good to have a nerd for a husband!

After lunch I watched Jerry shuttle backwards and forwards between the shed and the house, collecting the tools he was going to need. I sat and watched until the third metal ruler had disappeared into the house. I had my trusty e-reader and sat in the sun reading while the odd opening and closing of the shutters and windows went on. Then Jerry emerged from the house with a couple of glasses of fruit juice.

Jerry was smiling and whistling as he handed me a glass. Always a good sign.

"How is it going?" I ask, knowing the

answer will be positive.

"I've measured twice and got the same answers!" He smiled, "If it comes out the same next time, I'll cut the bits to fit and get on with putting the lot together."

He finished his drink and we chatted for a few minutes about my book. "It's a romance," I tell him. "A young policeman meets a trainee solicitor." I know my husband well, the moment I mentioned it was a romantic story he had switched off. Moments later he was off back to the house.

Half an hour later I hear the sound of metal being cut and drilled. Then the sound of Jerry's electric screwdriver. The noise went on for quite a while, then it happened.

"Yes!" Jerry shouted in triumph.

Then it went silent for a few minutes before the drilling and screwing started again. Jerry was obviously doing one window at a time. The second one took less time. The third one involved a lot more drilling and screwing. I got concerned about the amount of time it was taking. I put my book down and wandered back towards the house. Immediately I saw why it was taking more drilling for the final window. Jerry had sensibly left the French windows of our bedroom to last. Maybe that is why he has been successfully organising jobs for as long as I have known him.

Best to let him get on with it, the absence of swearing indicates things are still going well. As I walked back, the noise stopped. So, did I, listening.

"Yes!" All three appear to have passed the Jerry quality test. I reversed my direction of travel. A few minutes later I was offering my husband a chilled glass of beer as he was putting sealant into the gaps between the frame and the uneven stone of the window opening.

He demonstrated the windows opening and the shutters shutting with the insect screens moving up and down. He was very proud of what he had achieved. I was very pleased it had all gone so well.

That night we shut the shutters, pulled down the screens and left the windows open. A breeze blew through the bedroom and we slept, much better than we had for nights. I woke a couple of times listening out for that high-pitched

whine of biting bastards. Not a sound!
Wonderful!

The Last Battle

Fran tells me she didn't hear any mossies during the night. I did, I went downstairs for a drink about two o'clock and when I switched on the light there was a swarm of them buzzing around it. It was obvious to me that we would need to do all the windows and doors to keep them out. Even once they are all screened, there are times when we have to open the screens to get in and out. We need to thin out the number of beasts outside trying to get to feast on my blood!

What do I need to do to get rid of them, without us having to live in NBC suits, that's Nuclear, Biological and Chemical Warfare suits, for a month afterwards? I consult Mr Google. There were lots of results for dealing with the family Culicidae, as I discover the mosquito is part of and that there are some three and a half thousand species of mosquito. Mind you, only one hundred of them bite humans.

It did confirm a lot of what I already knew too. Water, stagnant, standing water is key to their life cycle. The other thing is long grass for hiding in.

Me and the MB had dealt with all the long grass over the past few weeks. I went on a hunt for standing water. I emptied bits of hose, flower pots and tin cans. I'm sure there wasn't enough water for the number of mossies we were getting. I could hear movement from next door, Ian might have experience of controlling the bastard beasties. I popped around to the house and rang the doorbell.

Ian answered a minute or so later and invited me into the front room. I explained my reason for calling and the steps I had taken so far in my quest to deal with the vampire insects.

Ian agreed that I had been doing the right things. He followed much the same regime and they didn't have a big problem with them. He had planted a few citronella and basil plants around the garden to deter the beasts as well.

"They can fly quite a way, have you checked the other side of the fence?" He suggested.

"That's why I'm here," I answered rather stupidly before the penny dropped! "The other side of our garden, of course, there is no one looking after it!"

After I left Ian to get back on with whatever he was doing, I walked to our other neighbours' house. The garden was a mess, weeds and grass up to my knees. Then I found the pool, half full of black water. I guessed I had found the source of our problem. Now, what to do. I knew that the Mighty Brushwhacker had a new mission. The pool was another issue. Time to consult Mr Google and Fran.

We all agreed very quickly that the garden had to be cut back. Fran suggested looking on Google Earth to see if there were any flower beds to be avoided. There was just a small border near the house, the summer before last, everything else appeared to be in pots and tubs. All systems go for Operation Brushwhacker.

The pool was a far trickier problem. We dared not drain it, as it might collapse inward, and in any case, it would refill once we had rain. The classic float a layer of oil on the surface would probably damage the sides of the pool and the filter when the pool was restarted. We were loath to use chemicals. There was only one solution left and it was a biological control.

The following morning while I was

whacking the weeds, Fran took the car to the local branch of Aqua-Jardin. Which is a garden centre that specialises in all things aquatic.

Our neighbours had left their garden relatively tidy compared to the tip we had found when we moved in. As a result, the Mighty Brushwhacker and I made great time. The cutting cord lasted ages and the grass and weeds were soon cut back to close to the recommended ten centimetres height. Fran had returned about half an hour earlier. Her purchases were safe on the sideboard, while we shared a cup of tea!

While she was out, Fran had popped into one of the more distant of our local shops and found fresh, un-heat-treated milk. We had a couple more cups of tea and we broke out the last packet of digestive biscuits to go with them. Heaven had come to our kitchen!

Before it started to get dark, we took Fran's Aqua-Jardin purchases next door. I lowered the one bag into the water and secured it to the steps. We then opened the other packages and spread out the contents. It looked like everything was present and correct.

I opened the bag and released the five goldfish into the pool. According to Mr G., they should munch their way through hundreds of mosquito larvae a day. That'll soon clear the pool as a breeding ground. We then pulled some netting over the pool and pegged it securely in place with the tent pegs Fran had bought. I looked at our handy work. I couldn't see a heron getting through the net to get our anti-mosquito fish!

Over the next week we noticed a marked reduction in the number of the biting beasts troubling us around the pool. I also fitted screens to all the windows of the house. We were sleeping better too, who needs noisy, expensive air conditioning.

The Big Reveal

Our party is tomorrow! Thankfully Teen and Ian have agreed to give a hand. Teen and I are in the kitchen, assembling all the cold dishes we can and prepping the ingredients for the dishes that will need to be served hot.

Jerry and Ian are out at the local wine store buying the beer and the wine. Hopefully, Ian will have moderated Jerry. He tends to forget to spit when he is tasting wines.

It was getting on towards mid-afternoon when the boys got back. They had bought several gallons of wine in boxes. We had agreed that this would be better than loads of bottles. Getting the rosé and white into the fridge alongside all of the food was tricky! The beer went into a large plastic dustbin we would be filling with ice and water tomorrow morning.

I was aware that both boys were slightly happy and relaxed, but they had worked hard, walking back and forth to and from the car with the boxes and cases. By the time they finished, they were both looking very hot. I'm not sure what happened next. I remember Teen shouting, "Skinny dip! The last one in's a rotter!" And we were all running towards the pool, pulling off our clothes. Jerry was the last one in, I think he was a little surprised by the arrival of Teen's shorts as she threw them into the air, hitting him on the chest as he struggled with the buttons on his shorts.

We were sitting on the sunbeds sipping wine and nibbling nuts, while Teen continued to insist she had said 'Cooling dip!'. The smile on Ian's face suggested that it might have been a pre-planned ploy to get us all undressed in the pool.

Then Ian put his glass down and asked a surprising question

"Your Aunt Gillian, you said she lives on a farm in Spain and does Bed and Breakfast?"

I'm confused, where is this coming from and where is it going to? I nod in response.

"Is her husband called Bill?"

I nodded again still unsure of what was going on.

"I think we might have stayed there, several years ago. It was well before we bought the house here."

"What a small world," I commented. Before I could follow that line of thought, we were all distracted.

"Heron!" Jerry was pointing to a thin, tall, grey bird sitting on a tree in the garden next door. "We were right to get that net."

"What net?" Teen and Ian asked, almost as one.

Jerry explained the goldfish, mosquito larvae and the anti-heron net we had put over the pool.

"You put goldfish into their swimming pool?" Teen was not quite up to speed.

"They will eat all the larvae and I don't see them doing any damage to the pool or the environment," Jerry explained proudly.

Since we were on the subject of our other neighbours, I thought it was time to find out more about them.

"What can you tell us about our other

neighbours? We haven't met them yet," I asked.

"Philipp und Krystianne, you're not likely to see them this year. I doubt if they will ever get to come here again. Philipp had a heart attack just before Christmas and Kyrstianne is almost totally immobile with her rheumatism." Teen shook her head sadly, "Such a shame, they were both such fun!"

"Especially after half a bottle of schnapps!" Ian chuckled, nodding in agreement with his wife."

"Ah, that explains why someone told us we might not be seeing them this summer! The gossip made it appear to be much darker." Deciding to go for broke I put the whole story out there. "We were at a village event back in the spring and Roger told us that we had naturists living next door," I explained.

I saw a strange look pass between Ian and Teen before Ian responded,

"That'll be us then! Philipp and Krystianne use to call us 'les voisins naturiste', that is the naturist neighbours to you and me! Roger must have heard them referring to us and got confused.

Typical ex-pat gossip, take a grain of truth and season it with exaggeration and misinformation and serve it up as a tasty titbit."

"We were wondering how to break the news to you. Once you had confirmed about Gillian and Bill, we knew we would have to tell you before she arrived for her visit and recognised us!

"You? You and Ian? You are our naturist neighbours?" I was flabbergasted, "You can't be! You are such normal people. I mean you are just like us."

"Of course, we are!" Teen had obviously experienced my reaction before. "We are normal people. The same number of arms, legs, eyes and noses as most other people. We eat, drink and breathe in the same way. At home I have to go to work in the morning, wearing clothes and come home in the evening still wearing them. All very normal."

While she paused for breath, Jerry asked the question. The one that had been worrying us since we had heard about our naturist neighbours.

"Does that mean you don't go in for

noisy, all night, drunken sex parties? You know, car keys in the fishbowl, naked Twister and copulating couples in the pool...that sort of thing?"

"No, Jerry," There was a weariness in Ian's voice, "We have parties, noisy parties, with lots of drink but we invite most of the ex-pats you've met, several of the local wine and food producers, Madame La Notaire, the Mayor and the guys of the Police Municipal. I hope you have invited them too?" I ran the mental checklist, yes, they were on our list. "Just to stay on their good side. We don't have a fishbowl and I can't imagine Jean-Jaques, (one of our local cheese producers, now in his eighties,) being able to reach the Twister mat!"

"It's not as if everything you read in the papers and online is all true," Teen picked up the narrative, leaving Ian shaking his head, trying to get the image of the one-twenty kilo cheese producer trying to play Twister out of his imagination.

She continued "We don't go around naked all the time, you have seen us in clothes. In fact, we wear them most of the time, less so in summer, but even then, we seldom manage a whole day clothing free. What with trips to the shop visitors and mosquitoes!"

"Mind you," Ian interjected, with a mischievous grin dancing on his lips, "We don't do swimwear, we don't own any ... What's it for? It doesn't keep you dry, it doesn't keep you warm, or cool, it certainly doesn't make you swim any better!"

"Modesty?" I volunteered.

"Like you now?" Teen asked looking at me with eyebrows raised.

I'd forgotten that we still bare following our earlier swim.

"Now tell me why you knew you would have to tell the tale before Gillian arrived? ... Oh, an alternative, bohemian lifestyle ..." I spluttered to a stop.

Then my mind raced on, I made a mental note to have a word with Gavin and Inga too. A word about them visiting Gillian's and why the pool had stayed clear during their visit.

But first, we shared a toast to our arrival 'Aperaty' tomorrow. After that our new lives officially begin and who knows what changes and new adventures lie ahead...

Tomorrow Fran and Jerry hold their Aperaty.

The enigmatic Aunty Gillian is coming to stay very soon.

How close to Chicago do John and Lauren live now?

What is going to happen to Philipp and Krystianne' s house?

Given a little persuasion and encouragement by way of your reviews I might write the second part of Jerry and Fran's adventures in rural France ...

Meet Ted Bun

I was born in London in 1956 and have lived most of my life in the South of England.

Ted Bun came into existence in 2005 with the launch of the website 'The Sun on Our Buns' (www.sunnybuns.me.uk). The pseudo-name was necessary because I was working for a large, national organisation and association with naturism may not have gone down well!

Strangely, although I know nothing about how computers work, my work at that time was mainly to do with IT projects. I suppose what I was doing was process redesign. Then we were reorganised and suddenly I found myself working as an independent contractor.

A few years later and independent contractors were all on the way out.

Looking in H&E Naturist one month, I saw an article/advert for a small naturist resort in Portugal that was available for rental. The ideal opportunity for Ted Bun to start his new career!

Three fun-filled summers later, Mrs Bun decided this was what we wanted to do. We then spent two years searching for the right house to leave the rat race behind. Then we found L'Olivette, our little piece of paradise in South West France, and we have started offering relaxing holidays by sharing our gîte our beautiful surroundings and our lives with people who love nature, all just 1km outside a vibrant, small town see it all at: www.handluggageholidays.co.uk

So, Ted Bun is:

> British,
> About 11 years old (still!),
> Married to Mrs Bun,
> Website author and designer, IT trainer,
> Owner of a small, friendly, naturist or clothing optional, holiday destination in beautiful SW France,
> Former Manager of the largest hard built naturist resort on the Algarve.

During the longer evenings of the quieter season, here in L'Olivette, a series of novellas and short stories started to take shape, 'The Rags to Riches' series.

The first book in which our central characters first meet, and romance starts, 'The Uncovered Policeman', was first published on Valentine's Day 2016.

You can e-mail me at:
ted.bun@sunnybuns.me.uk

Or follow my blog at www.tvhost.co.uk

Or why not come and share our little bit of paradise sometime soon?

Other books by Ted Bun:

Novellas

The Uncovered Policeman – Rags to Riches Book 1

The Uncovered Policeman Abroad – Rags to Riches Book 2

The Uncovered Policeman: In and Out of the Blues - Rags to Riches Book 3

The Uncovered Policeman: Goodbye Blues – Rags to Riches Book 4

Two Weddings and a Naming - Rags to Riches Book 5

The Uncovered Policeman: Caribbean Blues – Rags to Riches Book 6

The Uncovered Policeman: Family Album - Rags to Riches Book 7

A Spring Break at L'Abeille Nue - Rags to Riches Book 8

Short Stories

About Naturism

Naturism is the practice of going without clothes - whether that is just occasionally at a beach or in your garden, or as a more general part of everyday life. Naturism is healthy, sensible - who wants to wear clothes when the weather is hot – and great fun!

Naturism is normal

It's just ordinary people choosing not to wear clothes when the weather and circumstances are appropriate. Our activities are no different from what most people do in their leisure time, other than the dress code. We're not anti-clothes, we just know they are not always essential. It's also a lot of fun!

Naturism is not about sex

Naturists are not asexual, but despite what people think, a gathering of naked people doesn't make for a sexually charged environment.

You won't be embarrassed!

Once in a naturist place, you soon get used to being surrounded by naked people and forget that you are not wearing clothes. It's clothed people that stand out. What you look like is irrelevant. No-one stares at you, or judges your appearance – it's all about feeling good about yourself and your body, no matter what its shape, size or age. No-one is forced to be naked all the time and people will put something on if the weather turns colder.

Naturism is very popular

Millions of people in the UK and around the world have discovered this wonderful way of life. There are thousands of holiday resorts and other places serving the community. Plenty of people skinny-dip, go topless on beaches and spend time naked at home.

Naturist children are happy, well-adjusted and safe

Children don't care if they are wearing clothes or not, it's adults who make them get dressed. They grow up with a better understanding of what will happen to their bodies and enjoy a relaxed, outdoor life. Naturist places tend to have entry requirements and secure gates, making the inside a far safer environment than the outside.

Printed in Great Britain
by Amazon